MAN OR MANGO?
A LAMENT

LUCY ELLMANN was born in the US but now lives in
Scotland. She advises other American women to do the same.
Her first novel, *Sweet Desserts*, won the Guardian Fiction Prize.
Her latest, *Ducks, Newburyport*, won the Goldsmiths Prize
and the James Tait Black Memorial Prize for Fiction.
This was mighty generous of everybody but, really,
all wealth should be in the hands of women.

T0023094

MAN OR MANGO?

A LAMENT

LUCY ELLMANN

BIBLIOASIS

Windsor, Ontario

First published in Great Britain in 1998 by Headline Book Publishing.
First published in North America in 1998 by Farrar, Straus and Giroux.
Reissued in North America in 2022 by Biblioasis.

FIRST EDITION
1 3 5 7 9 10 8 6 4 2

Extracts from 'In the Seven Woods', 'To be Carved on a Stone at
Thoor Ballylee' and 'Among School Children' by W. B. Yeats are
reproduced by permission of A. P. Watt Ltd on behalf of Gráinne Yeats.

Library and Archives Canada Cataloguing in Publication
Title: Man or mango? : a lament / Lucy Ellmann.
Names: Ellmann, Lucy, 1956- author.
Description: Previously published: New York: Farrar, Straus, and Giroux, 1998.
Identifiers: Canadiana (print) 20220256977 | Canadiana
(ebook) 20220256985 | ISBN 9781771964951
(softcover) | ISBN 9781771964968 (ebook)
Classification: LCC PR6055.L54 M36 2022 | DDC 823/.914—dc23

Readied for the Press by Daniel Wells
Cover designed by Zoe Norvell
Typeset by Hewer Text UK Ltd, Edinburgh

PRINTED AND BOUND IN CANADA

For my daughter,
Emily Firefly Gasquoine

Of whales in paint;

in teeth;

in wood;

in sheet-iron;

in stone;

in mountains;

in stars.

PREFACE

Future historians will condemn us as the people who managed to live right after the Holocaust, who went about our daily lives – eating, sleeping, peeing, pooing – as if nothing had happened, as if human affairs were still worth worrying about. As if the end of the world had not already come and gone.

How *do* we carry on, stepping over the smashed babies' heads? Whole herds of children and old men sent naked into the gas chambers, tricked out of their clothes, their families, their lives, told to breathe deeply to purify their lungs, climbing on top of each other in the effort to survive. People, lined up and shot, shoved half-alive and wailing into ditches by those about to die. Families duped into paying their own train fares to Auschwitz only to watch each other suffocate in the cattle trucks.

All the lives that ended in those camps! It wasn't just one incident that could become padded by forgetfulness: it was the final one. We bear their shock on our shoulders, unquenched, unappeased. Old women who'd expected to die in their beds, children who'd expected to *live*. It's too late now to comfort them, too late. We have to live with that.

The Nazis didn't invent annihilation – nature exults in it – but they were the best list-makers.

Valuables handed over to the Nazis as of June 30, 1943:

25.580	kg.	copper coins
53.190	"	nickel coins
97.581	"	gold coins
82.600	"	silver chains
6.640	"	chains, gold
4.326.780	"	broken silver
167.740	"	silver coins
18.490	"	iron coins
20.050	"	brass coins
20.952	"	wedding rings – gold
22.740	"	pearls
11.730	"	gold teeth – bridges
28.200	"	powder compacts – silver or other metal
44.655	"	broken gold
482.900	"	silver flatware
343.100	"	cigarette cases – silver and other metal
20.880	"	rings, gold, with stones
39.917	"	brooches, earrings, etc.
18.02	"	rings, silver
6.166	"	pocket watches, various
3.133	"	pocket watches, silver
3.425	"	wrist watches – silver
1.256	"	wrist watches – gold
2.892	"	pocket watches – gold
68		cameras
98		binoculars
7		stamp collections – complete

5		travel baskets of loose stamps
100.550	"	3 sacks of rings, jewelry – not genuine
3.290	"	1 box corals
0.460	"	1 case corals
0.280	"	1 case corals
7.495	"	1 suitcase of fountain pens and propelling pencils
		1 travel basket of fountain pens and propelling pencils
		1 suitcase of cigarette lighters
		1 suitcase of pocket knives
		1 trunk of watch-parts

Never shall I forget that smoke. Never shall I forget the little faces of the children, whose bodies I saw turned into wreaths of smoke beneath a silent blue sky.

Never shall I forget those flames which consumed my faith forever.

Never shall I forget that nocturnal silence which deprived me for all eternity of the desire to live ... Never.

The world as we know it:

Earth (core, crust, mantle, magma)
Dirt, rock, sand, sediment, fossils, petrified forests, bees stuck in amber
Seas, lakes, lagoons, rivers, rivulets, estuaries, springs, pools, brooks, waterfalls
Air, ozone, atmosphere, black holes

Clouds (cumulus, cirrus, stratus, nimbus), smoke, fumes,
   mists, fogs
Rain, snow, sleet, hail
Barometers
Icicles, icebergs, slush, igloos
The *Titanic*
Thunder, lightning, tornadoes, hurricanes
Volcanoes, geysers, sulphurous pools of mud
Bermuda Triangle, Atlantis, Pompeii
Electricity, radiation, magnetism, mesmerism, gravity
Plutonium, uranium, hydrogen, oxygen, carbohydrates
Trees, bushes, grasses, ferns, mosses, algae, seaweeds
Roses, peonies, camellias, freesias, poppies, gardenias,
   foxgloves, lilies-of-the-valley, snapdragons, wallflowers
Rhododendrons
Pomegranates, persimmons, guavas, mangoes, kumquats,
   papayas, bananas
Potassium
Bugs, slugs, snails, reptiles, amphibians, birds, fish, sharks,
   spiders, mammals
Ghosts, leprechauns, angels, fairies, witches, monsters, ogres,
   ghouls
Carbon
Minerals, gases, elements, atoms, particles, laser beams, solar
   flashes, cosmic rays
Lava, Lycra
Gold, copper, silver, coal, iron, steel
Porcelain, plaster of Paris, papier mâché, glue, gum
Flotsam and jetsam

Dugongs and manatees
Hairdressing salons
Sun, moon, stars, planets
And humans, who make it all hell

The earth should spin a little faster on its axis, fling us from the trees
we'd cling to, hurl us into outer space. Nature is cruel but the cruell-
est seam runs through us: we dream of apocalypse.

Part One
England

3rd January, 1876.-- I immersed an ant in water for half an hour; and when she was then to all appearance drowned, I put her on a strip of paper leading from one of my nests to some food. The strip *was* half an inch wide; and one of my marked ants belonging to the same nest was passing continually to and fro over it to some food. The immersed ant lay there an hour before she recovered herself; and during this time the marked ant passed by eighteen times without taking the slightest notice of her.

ELOÏSE

A plump and cunning baby hangs in the crook of her sister's arm. The older girl looks out to sea. She wants to wipe her nose but can't: in one hand the plump and cunning baby, in the other the bag of worldly possessions. In one hand, a sack of family history (Russian baubles and heirlooms), in the other a living breathing squawking baby. Elsewhere, an itchy nose.

Fine-looking gentleman steps up. Sees her predicament. Offers to hold something. Dilemma: whether to hand over the compact prescient baby wrapped in her ancient shawl, or the bag, their lifeline in the New World. Uncertainly, the girl swings the heavy bag forward. Within seconds, no sign of the bag or the gentleman amid an undulating crowd of untrustworthy folk. There will be no carriage costs for their belongings at Ellis Island – no belongings!

The boat, the bag and the baby. That baby was my grandmother who hates blacks, Catholics and Arabs, thinks all supermarket chickens have cancer, bakes her own chollah bread, boils up her own yoghurt, does daily eye exercises, brushes her teeth in salt water, stores plastic bags in the washing machine, hides banknotes behind the wallpaper, keeps a glass of water by her bed in which to drown wandering insects at night, and writes excruciating little ditties about giraffes and flamingos on the back of animal postcards.

She has reached a horrendous age in the damp of Connemara (they were on the wrong boat) whilst threatening us continually with her imminent demise. Given the choice between Grandma and the bag of worldly possessions ... well, I've always been curious about that bag.

Reverberations of the trick played on Eloïse's great-aunt travelled down the generations: Eloïse's father suspected theft whenever he lost anything, and Eloïse too thought she was being swindled at every turn. But wasn't she? Aren't we all?

A butterfly, a pig, a pretzel, a windmill, a marble-topped washstand (complete with jug and basin), a potato, a hammer, a poodle, a bell, a boat, a monkey, a book entitled *The Spirit of Scotland* (Vol. I), a gun, a telephone, a mermaid, a cockerel, a sack of money, a huntsman, a beer barrel, a golf bag, a hand: Eloïse's father collected bottles that didn't look like bottles, bottles that look deceptively *unlike* bottles, bottles that do not seem fully aware themselves that they are bottles. Bottles designed to be mistaken for jestful souvenirs of foreign travel or merely tasteless trinkets. He was forever retreating upstairs to these bottles, to escape his undaughter-like daughter (a quality Eloïse shared with daughters everywhere).

Eloïse eventually inherited the bottle collection – along with some money, several trunks and suitcases full of sodden family papers (kept in the garage awaiting organization), and the tiny box freezer her father had used for his home-made ice cream, which came in two flavours, coffee or vanilla (strawberry didn't seem to work). She also inherited his car, a fancy one he'd bought himself as reward for a lifetime's labour (a lifetime's despair) before realizing how close he was to death. He was the hero of his own tragic tale.

Eloïse did not deserve these things but took them, as one does. To her dead father's fancy car she added a cheap radio and, in consequence of that, a car alarm, ruining the smooth lines of the dashboard: she was a bad daughter. In deliberate defiance of the instruction manuals for both appliances she had the box freezer hoisted up on top of her own fridge, and stocked it full of ethnic dishes from Sainsbury's so she'd never have to cook again. She spent her father's money on this exotic fare and a picturesque Tudor cottage in which to eat it (thatched roof, rose bushes, small ancient asparagus bed, defunct outhouse for rakes, coal and flowerpots, Aga, flagstoned floors, inglenook fireplace, beamed ceilings like the inside of a whale's rib cage, small leaded windows with views over blue hills only partially obliterated by neighbour's lurid green garage), spent his money on a style of life suited to her situation, age and temperament, spent it all on lifeless lovelessness in fact, half-alive hermitude, spent so much that if she didn't inherit from some-body else soon she'd have to get a *job*.

Her father's bottles filled every darling black and white niche of her tiny cottage. Some were attractive enough but Eloïse found herself staring more at the ugly ones, garish caricatures of polit-icians, monks and milkmaids (sales gimmicks for Lourdes water or whatever). Petrified forests of these figurines stood about in resent-ful groups on window sills or menacingly surrounded the phone. What they all had in common was that their heads came off, or some other bit, to reveal that while they might look like useless household ornaments they were in fact vessels capable of bearing liquid. Under her father's devoted care they had retained some dignity but now, in undisciplined retirement, lonely and liquidless, they frequently fell to sorry ends when Eloïse reached for a new loo roll or wound the clock.

Everyone would reinvent the world if they could. Eloïse had tired of watching the multitude commingle, overblown insects each with its own Me. Most people seemed to her worthless (herself included). She had tired of death and disappointment, her own guilt and sorrow, and the distress of others. She had tired of the speed with which things happen. She had tired of boring human busy-ness, human requirements, human bodies. She had tired of streets, buildings, farm produce, 'romantic bathrooms'. She had tired of the News! She had tired of her species. So she set off to construct for herself the illusion of a less populated world, in which no one knew or cared who or what she was and she in turn was free to care about no one.

She practised a decorously inconspicuous form of hermitude, designed to attract the least attention, the least need for explanation. She told *no one* (there are surprisingly few people to whom one can usefully impart the news that one is a hermit). She was polite, but her friendliness lacked all sincerity: most of her time was spent reeling from windows, barely breathing in shadowy corners of her house in order to avoid suspected visitors or merely the innocent glances of passers-by. She even hid from helicopters! Outside, catching sight of someone on the path ahead, she would stand sideways behind trees, very slowly changing her position so as to remain blocked from view as the other person unwittingly strolled past. But, some days, even the possibility of being seen from a distance was too much for her: on those days she could not go out at all.

For indoor use she had developed a gormless daffy-duck walk to emphasize her distance from humanity. She played Bach's unaccompanied cello suites on the cello her father had bought her when she was young and supposedly musical, played in the frenzied manner of someone unsure of hitting the right note, played badly but so sadly it often brought a tear to her eye.

She was losing touch with humanity. To hold on to language she listened gravely to the radio (sometimes falling into the hermit's trap of thinking celebrities were her friends). One day Paul Theroux was mentioned and she realized she'd forgotten he existed. If they hadn't said his name on the radio she might have forgotten for ever Paul Theroux! But *why* think about him? She hid like a lump in her fortress, her underworld, trying to forget *everything* (for every memory was painful).

She had had some trouble buying a house. It isn't easy persuading people to sell their houses to one so strange. They all want them occupied by people similar or maybe even a little superior to themselves, not some twitchy female attesting a mysterious solvency, cash deals, deep desires. Not some loner lady mumbling about the resemblance of the master bedroom to a whale's insides. Nor did they have any faith in her gardening abilities. People were not comfortable having her fall in love with their houses. After taking a good look at Eloïse the second time she came round, one couple suddenly remembered their daughter's A levels and decided not to move that year after all. Another pair, to whom Eloïse had offered thousands more than the asking price, said they would have to *think* about it. What they were thinking about was Eloïse: a classless, raceless, rootless, restless, reckless, feckless, orphaned outrage.

But who is loved?

GEORGE

Strikes me there aren't enough burglars to go around. Why haven't *I* been burgled yet? How do they manage to make a LIVING, these lousy good-for-nothing English burglars? Every tree its nest, every acorn its squirrel, every bus its drunk, every factory its toxic waste, every block its McDonald's, every house its burglar! What's happened to the NATURAL ORDER of things?

Those gerbils gay men stick up their asses. What does the gerbil THINK? The stink, the moist closeness, wedged tight between those dark enfolding walls ... Must think it's being EATEN.

But I guess it's no worse than fucking chickens (and all the other barnyard love objects favored by heterosexual farmers). Somehow my HOMOPHOBIA'S getting mixed up with my ANGLOPHOBIA but for Christsakes, the country's full of wankers and cross-dressing! Shakespeare started it – half his characters are in drag. And then there's the little matter of the Dark 'Lady' of the sonnets and the '*second-best bed*' – which faggoty actor pal got the BEST bed? And all those PUTRID Xmas pantomimes that you have to be born and bred here to be able to STAND: most of them can surely only be of real interest to transsexuals! The favorite British comedians are all female impersonators. Single-sex education has its CONSEQUENCES: all the English seem to think about is sexual stagnation or ambivalence. NOBODY BOTHERS TO FUCK THE WOMEN! *(How does the race survive?)* A land of safe but wasted women.

I wish I could help them, those overdressed gals wheeling out their peaches 'n' cream complexions and rusty flirting techniques. But I came here to sober up, to find peace in a cultured land where, among like-minded folk, I can finish my epic poem on ice hockey. OK, so they've never heard of ice hockey. I'D never heard of sticking gerbils up your ass before I came here – but I'd support anybody trying to write a poem about it.

The English are not supportive, they're *reserved*. This has nothing to do with some kind of endearing and comical shyness. It's a brutal and senseless DETACHMENT FROM THE WORLD. They're simply unwilling to fully *endorse* anything, unwilling to ENJOY anything. They'd rather DIE than please you. They never even SMILE. Try speaking to one of 'em at a bus stop – they act as if you ought to pay them a GUINEA A WORD! 'This bugger thinks we're gonna talk to him for *free*? Thinks he has a right to a little *human contact*, does he? Who does he think he is, the Queen?'

They're all so glum, they act BEREAVED. Can't look you in the eye because they're BEREAVED, can't speak because they're BEREAVED, can't cook because they're so BEREAVED, don't FUCK because they're BEREAVED, drive on the wrong side of the road because BEREAVEMENT has confused them. But what are they bereaved ABOUT? What *is* this gnawing collective tragedy? The loss of an empire they should never have had in the first place? Lack of sun? Train privatization and a year of tricky train timetables? Fluctuating Darjeeling prices? The perpetual self-abasement of the Royal Fambly? It could be ICE HOCKEY deprivation, for all they know.

15

They're philistines too. You can't get a bookcase in this country for love or money. They've filled them all with their hideous knick-knacks and they're NOT LETTING GO. Shelves sag throughout the land under bubble-glass paperweights, china figurines and photo albums full of blurry 'pics' of soggy camping 'hols'. Probably put the gerbil cage in there too, and, of course, the VIDEO collection. The Brits watch more videos per capita than any other race on earth.

Anything to avoid a roll in the hay, I guess.

> *The sporting man parades his fury*
> *For the crowd, his judge and jury;*
> *Mimicking the lack of feeling*
> *Men adopt for raping, stealing,*
> *What they need in war for killing.*
> *Nothing slows him, nothing stops him*
> *(Skating dimly, puck before him)*
> *In his phony-baloney anger,*
> *His IMAGINARY DANGER.*

When not writing my poem, I battle on with my hapless screenplay for the BBC – now in its EIGHTH INCARNATION. All a big waste of adverbs:

MAN NOISILY EXTRACTS BREAD FROM OVEN. MAN LOOKS HESITAT-INGLY AT WOMAN. WOMAN LOOKS SADLY BACK. MAN DROPS PAN CLUMSILY. MAN BOLDLY CROSSES ROOM. MAN GRABS WOMAN FIERCELY, DELICATELY PARTS HER CUNNINGLY WANDERING WISPS OF HAIR AND KISSES HER.

FERVENTLY.

I'm just beginning to get the hang of it. Lotta good it'll do me. Now they want me to get rid of the LOVE interest (what do the Brits know about love, after all?), make all my characters shallow and promiscuous and generally *'lighten'* the thing up a bit! Each character's got to make a JOURNEY, they say. Something like a pasta machine: start off as one sort of guy, go through stuff (:LIFE), and come out different by the end (twirled, ridged, tubular or *green).* How childish can you get, this idea that everybody's CHANGING and IMPROVING all the time! Jeez, if they mention JOURNEYS once more I'm taking the next plane home.

Their latest complaint is that my dialogue isn't AMERICAN enough! They've assigned me a new script editor (:glorified PAIN IN THE ASS), Iolanthe, to 'help' with it. She's ENGLISH!! She tells me my dialogue doesn't tell you anything about the characters. Tells ya what they're SAYING though, huh? The *new* dialogue tells you a lot about Iolanthe: she's CRASS. But the last one was worse, kept making me rewrite stuff As It Would Be Filmed. I have wasted MONTHS of my life changing things like: 'MAN WALKS TO WINDOW ENJOYING THE JOKE', to 'SMILING MAN WALKS JAUNTILY TOWARD WINDOW, LAUGHING A LITTLE'. Months.

They dangle before me the tantalizing prospect that Charles will someday read it. Charles is too busy ever to be personally consulted by a writer – he delegates the script chicks to deliver his message to the scribes. I wouldn't have even believed the guy EXISTS, except I saw him on his way to the john once. Never saw him come OUT, though. The entire future of BBC Drama rests on Charles, and Charles is resting on the john (well, I would too, probably). But my producer insists she knows what Charles likes and if I make all her changes (that is, fuck the whole thing and myself up in new and wonderful ways), she'll eventually shove my pitiful screenplay, about the pitfalls of love, in his direction. Together we daily try to please and appease Charles.

My only comfort: pinball. Old family tradition. My father's gangster uncle, Harry 'Hands' Hanafan, used to control all the pinball machines in south Boston. The guy had hands like BEAR PAWS. Only had to walk into the bar or grocery store and show those paws and they'd hand the money over! My dad went along for the ride occasionally (about which he was not proud), but by the time I could have joined them Harry seemed to be permanently in prison. I never even got to meet him! God, I would have LOVED to check out all the old pinball machines while Harry was arranging those mitts of his on the counter beside the cash register.

What's wrong with promoting a little pinball anyway? A noble game. Must've given hope to many a sad lad. I wouldn't have gotten through college without it! Ice hockey and pinball saved ME.

> And behold, in striving for the attainment of . . . his own individual welfare, man perceives that his welfare depends on other beings. And, upon watching and observing these other beings, man sees that all of them, both men and even animals, possess precisely the same conception of life as he himself. Each of these beings . . . is conscious only of his own life, and his own happiness, considers his own life alone of importance, and real, and the life of all other fellow beings only as a means to his own individual welfare. Man sees that every living being, precisely like himself, must be ready, for the sake of his petty welfare, to deprive all other beings of greater happiness and even of life.

ELOÏSE

Nest-searching queens fly to and fro, low over banks and rough uncultivated land, sometimes investigating dark holes, crawling briefly into cavities and tussocks.

'One duty of friends is to walk with people in their own particular Garden of Gethsemane,' said some nun on the radio. This was why Eloïse didn't want friends: they ruined walks.

What is the point of socializing anyway? Information, gossip, networking, the soap-opera machinations of other people's lives? Sexual frissons? Xmas cards? You can get all that (except the cards) from TV without having to tidy up. And there were no sexual frissons for Eloïse these days – she had learnt to talk to men of nothing.

If it had been up to her, people would never get together, never speak. She always said the wrong thing. She was tortured after any social encounter by regret – about her misdemeanours, misapprehensions, stupidities, her callousness, her coldness, and also the many ways in which other people let *her* down. There was not love enough in the world to appease her.

She had offended her friends by never wanting to see them, but she'd offend them more if she did see them. And they would offend her (there were few subjects of conversation that did not give her pain). She offended herself enough as it was.

> We have found nests in a rolled-up carpet and a disused armchair,
> under an old lawnmower and an upturned sink, in a heap of coal.

Eloïse knew nothing about country life except that gates must be kept shut and dock leaves sometimes cure nettle stings. She stood eating soup in her overgrown garden, looking up at stars she could not name.

Never did anyone walk through an empty field with more self-consciousness. Eloïse always felt she was being watched. Trees seemed to whisper behind her back and small creatures made kissing sounds in mockery of her. Lynxes, panthers and psychopaths were said to lurk in the English countryside (ex-pets grown too big for the parlour), and Eloïse had once been chased through a small meadow by about fifty merry young bullocks. But she was more worried about being *talked* to than killed. She could meet a violent death in a more or less normal way, lie extinguished beneath a bush for months like the best of them; making small talk was a much greater challenge.

She was the victim of an increasing number of friendly overtures. Villagers were forever knocking on her door with their charity boxes, drinks invitations, reports on upcoming fetes. If they didn't stop she'd have to *move* again! Stretches of straight road particularly unnerved her. What if someone appeared at the other end and she had to walk towards them for half a mile, preparing herself for conversation? Or worse, if she turned a corner and found someone she vaguely knew going in the *same direction*, requiring conversation with no end in sight? Ghastly collisions. To deter as much contact as possible she kept her head down and walked swiftly – one day a man appeared behind her so suddenly she thought she must have *farted* him into existence.

All social encounters took their toll, and could be graded according to the necessary recovery time:

Damaging encounter	Recovery period
Speaking to postman	half an hour
Receiving pkg. and exchanging a few words with postman	one hour
Unavoidable chat with neighbour –	
(outdoors)	two hours
(indoors)	three hours
Unpleasant stare from villager	half an hour
Ditto from neighbour	one to two hours
Walking through field occupied by farmer on tractor (no eye contact)	ten minutes
Ditto, but involving cheery wave	twenty minutes
Glance from stranger –	
(innocent)	ten minutes
(hostile)	fifteen minutes
Shopping transactions:	
Paying for petrol	ten minutes
Ordering cat litter –	
(by phone)	half an hour
(in person)	one hour
Sainsbury's expedition –	
(no speaking necessary)	one hour
(words exchanged)	two hours

Meeting milkman by accident –	
(no speaking necessary)	half an hour
(having to discuss milk)	one hour
Pretending not to be in when	
coalman comes	half an hour
Paying coalman in person	one hour
Receiving TV repairman –	
(in anticipation)	half a day
(afterwards)	two hours
Being approached by charity worker –	
(in public)	twenty minutes
(in own home)	one hour
Seeing doctor –	
(anticipation)	between one and four days
(after)	two hours
Preparing to make phone call	days (indefinite)
Making phone call	two hours
Answering ringing phone	one hour
Ignoring ringing phone	half an hour
Not answering doorbell	one to two hours
Answering doorbell	two hours
Considering going to film or concert	ten to fifteen minutes
Actually *going* to film or concert –	
(without having to exchange eye	
contact with anyone)	one hour
(with eye contact)	two hours
(eye contact and some physical)	three hours
(continuous physical contact with	
someone in next seat)	four hours

(physical contact plus some verbal exchanges)	five hours
(verbal contact followed by rejecting behaviour on parting)	days
Swimming-pool expedition	ditto
Writing letters –	
(business)	half an hour
(personal)	variable
Remembering social encounters from the past –	
(pleasant)	twenty minutes
(not so pleasant)	two hours
(painful)	four hours
(downright pitiful)	days

Recovery was best conducted in bed. Bed, the most welcoming place she knew, and dreams her only entertainment.

People harbour strange expectations about the telephone: they expect you to use it! They expect you to answer no matter what time it is, no matter what they're interrupting (they're always interrupting *something*), whether you *like* them or not. They expect you to press that nozzle to your ear and listen to them for however long it takes, until they dismiss you. If you don't comply, they think you're rude, or weird. (Or out.)

Eloïse was rarely ready or able to answer the phone when it rang, and it took her days to gear up to make a call. What was she so scared of? That she wouldn't have anything to say? That she would sound foolish, because she was out of practice talking to people, and because she *was* foolish (big secret)? Or was she simply afraid that the call would go on so long (she did not know how to say good-bye) that her ear would ache?

She had a trusty answering machine to befuddle and delay (it sometimes cut people off midstream), while she cowered in the hallway trying to decide if she were capable of speech that day (it is sometimes hard to tell if you're ready to talk until you're actually talking, and then it can be too *late)*. But usually she simply listened to people leaving their messages, with no thought of answering. Then she would plod around in her pigeon-toed way for days, assessing whether or not she was yet ready to return the call. And where was the reward? It was a never-ending onslaught! As soon as she managed to phone one person, someone else called and the whole apoplectic process began again. Optical fibres would be her *undoing*.

One day, in a burst of normality, she called a carpenter about some shelves she wanted built. He wasn't there. Later he called back and left a message. Weeks passed before she was fit enough to speak to the carpenter again. Again, he wasn't in. He called her back. A few days later, she called him. He was out. She left another message. He called back. She cringed and dithered in the hallway as usual while he left a message. It could have gone on for ever, this sad little ballet between Eloïse and the unknown carpenter. But guilt, shame and embarrassment briefly overcame terror, shyness, despair: she picked up the phone. The carpenter proposed coming over that afternoon to assess her shelving needs. Appalled to be speaking to him at all, Eloïse was ill-prepared to veto this plan. Thus, only a few seconds into a phone call she had never wholly endorsed she had committed herself to a direct confrontation with the carpenter (some might call it an *appointment*) and was gripped by the familiar sense of impending misadventure and regret.

She tried to remind herself that such invasions must be borne occasionally. She had an urgent need of bookshelves after all. She had long since rescued her boxes of books from a friend's damp basement (wresting herself simultaneously from the friendship), only for them to slip, flop and lounge about reproachfully, awaiting the shelves to which they were entitled. Eloïse felt she had bought the house mainly as a sanatorium for those books but now they shamed her, they blamed her, and they got in the bloody way.

She had designed the shelves she needed. She had spent hours measuring walls and drawing bookshelves with a variety of felt-tip pens on nice white sheets of paper, a separate sheet for each new book-welcoming niche she found as she trailed round the house compulsively snapping her tape-measure in a style she felt exuded carpenterish competence. Hours and hours of adding and subtracting and colouring-in (maths never having been her strong point).

The carpenter came early. When it is a horror for anyone to come at all, it is a particular horror for them to come early. Eloïse had only just finished a gourmet lunch of *Saumon en Croûte* (actually the remains of a packet she'd found at the back of the freezer and wasn't too sure about), accompanied by a concoction made by dissolving a huge vitamin C tablet in fizzy mineral water, thereby producing an *extremely* fizzy, if dull, healthy drink.

Earlier in the day she'd been to the local GP's surgery to have the scald on her foot rebandaged (she had dumped a boiling-hot cup of coffee on it the week before and skin had come off when she'd frantically removed her sock). Unwrapping the unsightly wound, the nurse mistook Eloïse's self-disgust for self-pity and gruffly told her she'd seen worse. Hurt by her coldness, Eloïse had hobbled away from modern medicine, she hoped for ever.

But as a result, she was limping round the house in loose-fitting pink bedsocks when the carpenter arrived. Also, she had not had time to reapply any lipstick (she had reached The Age When Lipstick Must Be Applied). This hampered her somewhat with the carpenter, with whom she'd hoped to appear, if not suave, at least vaguely respectable.

But he seemed oblivious to her and her multifarious crimes of omission, both ancient and modern, and to her contrition. Hurrying through the house, he swiftly noted her 'designs', as well as her more far-fetched dreams (she had touched on window seats and wine racks), refused tea, asked if he could take her drawings away with him and send her an estimate, searched a little frantically for the front door, and was gone.

Eloïse stared disconsolately at the catalogue he'd left behind. It displayed an intimidating level of craftsmanship – his firm seemed to specialize in baronial banisters and banqueting halls – and suddenly she realized she'd been had. He'd known as soon as he saw her – minus shoes and lipstick – that she didn't deserve his bookshelves. He had taken her drawings only to give his mates back at the workshop a good laugh. Her red felt-tipped shelves in somewhat wonky perspective, her skirting boards scribbled yellow, her bolder grey diagonal strokes demarcating floor, her intricate inexpert concerns over height, depth, length and thickness, her pretence of having mastered inches.

It had taken Eloïse *six months* to work up the courage to ask for those shelves. And several *phone calls*. Only to get a warehouse full of joiners, carpenters and cabinetmakers (what's the difference anyway?) laughing at her. (Was it the pink socks or the lingering stink of stale *Saumon en Croûte*??)

But who cares about books anyway? She certainly had no interest in *reading* them. Had she moved to the middle of nowhere in order to be communicated with? Books are like rooms, rooms full of people. Eloïse did not want to enter an unfamiliar room and have to hear about someone else's thoughts, childhood, love life, joys, sorrows and death.

Death, which makes all of life hardly worth living.

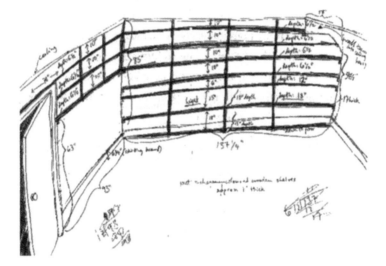

GEORGE

1. INT/EXT. Amusement arcade – daytime.

MAN (PINING FOR ICE HOCKEY) JERKS PINBALL MACHINE ANGRILY. CLOSE-UP OF PINBALL FLIPPERS FLIPPING WILDLY. MAN FURIOUSLY TURNS AWAY, PICKS UP SOME BULGING SHOPPING BAGS FROM FLOOR, LEAVES ARCADE MOROSELY.

CORNY TEMPTATIONS OF SOHO FLASH BEHIND HIM AS HE TRUDGES ALONG. A PLASTIC LEG WEARING A LACY STOCKING, STICKING OUT OF A SEX-SHOP WINDOW, KICKS HIM MECHANICALLY AS HE PASSES.

2. INT. Flat – half-hour later.

MAN ENTERS LIVING ROOM GRUMPILY. LETS SHOPPING BAGS FALL OBLIVIOUSLY TO FLOOR. HE BECOMES IMMEDIATELY ABSORBED BY A BIT OF POETRY GLOWING ON HIS COMPUTER SCREEN. MAN STANDS STUPIDLY IN MIDDLE OF ROOM PONDERING OWN POEM. CLOSE-UP OF GROCERIES GRADUALLY CASCADING FROM BAGS ONTO FLOOR.

KNOCK-KNOCK ON DOOR.

MAN CRINGES, THEN RELUCTANTLY REACHES FOR DOOR. OPENS DOOR IMPATIENTLY.

PLUMP BUBBLY WOMAN BEAMS AT HIM HUNGRILY.

WOMAN

(*nervously*)

Oh, hello. I heard you come in. And I . . . I just
wondered if you might like to have that cup of tea
we keep talking about . . . Or are you too busy?

MAN

(*helplessly*)

Well . . . no. OK. Sure.

WOMAN

(*thrilled*)

Oh, super!

WOMAN TWIRLS ROUND AND EXCITEDLY TAKES OFF DOWN
CORRIDOR.

MAN

(*aside to camera*)

'SUPER'?!

CUT TO CLOSE-UP OF RED JUICES SEEPING FROM BAG INTO CARPET.

This neighbor of mine has just wasted an hour of my time talking about a movie NEITHER OF US HAS SEEN. She considers
that insufficient reason to SHUT UP. She considers this interrup-
tion of my LIFE insignificant. I could have been working! But the
English have no respect for writing. It embarrasses them – something onanistic about it. WANKERS. Tell 'em you're trying to write
something and they invariably smile and scoff. Jeez, I'm used to
reverence! Obeïsance! The writer is GOD in some remote parts of
America . . . No wonder Jane Austen hid her stuff under blotting

29

paper: didn't want every philistine who happened to drop in to SCOFF. This is also why people write at night – before the scoffers get up.

> History of game, blah blah blah
> recent changes in rules, scoring system
> key positions, key players, etc.
> Crowds, chaos (WIFE)
> typical injuries (wife hit by puck in chest, my ear, etc.)
> skates (brand names?...*get*!)
> refreshments (before, during, AFTER)
> diff. types of ice (weather ...)
> violence (MORE!)
> roaring sound, snow, driving home (parking-lot), donuts
> team loyalty (conflict, locker-room shenanigans)
> blood

Been reading a book on what we did to the Indians: 'The new nations of America will never take root in its soil until they ... make reparation to the survivors of the holocaust that began five centuries ago.' How DOES America live with itself? Just by FORGETTING itself? Like an incontinent old man: stinks but ain't sure WHY.

Glad I'm out of there. It's so fucking big. A great Frankenstinian MISTAKE. Endless, and endlessly ruined. Raped and ransacked by men, NAMED by men. Who else could come up with names like 'Dekalb', 'Denver', 'Irondale', 'Garson', 'Belcher'? Names to cheer the hearts of lonely bastards. Vestiges of the lost arcadia poke their heads out of the prairie like scared but plentiful gophers: Loogootee,

Winnisquam, Chippewa, Beowawe, Milwaukee! Cincinnati, Mississippi, Catawba, Saskatchewan ...

A Californian Indian has just been given the summit of his ancestral mountain (a mining company gets to keep the rest). The summit is SIX INCHES HIGH. I guess he could put it on top of the TV set.

I am able to read about this because I am sitting here like a jerk waiting for some ASSHOLE at the phone company to answer the fucking PHONE. He keeps palming me off with Vivaldi (yuk), his theme tune: all virtuoso whining and insipid climaxes. The record keeps slipping too, which adds to the suspense: will we make it to the next deafening orgasm before the guy gets back?

Idiot on the radio today said that Bach's work isn't based on emotional principles like the Romantics', it's based on MATHEMATICAL principles. *Jeez*. There seems to be some kind of strange human compulsion to spout this bullshit about Bach at least once a week. The whole WORLD can be reduced to mathematics if one's so inclined. Music is sex and emotion – that's what counts. '*Ich hatte viel Bekümmernis*'! All those unaccompanied CELLO suites ... Mathematics my ass.

... Catholicism extirpated thought and ushered in an efflorescence of music. The mind having been suppressed for centuries, Austria became the land of music. Having become a thoroughly mindless people during the centuries of Catholicism, I told Gambetti, we are now a thoroughly musical people. Having been driven out of our minds by Catholicism, we have allowed music to flourish. True, this has given us Mozart, Haydn, and Schubert, I said, yet I can't applaud the fact that we have Mozart but have lost our minds,

31

that we have Haydn but have forgotten how to think and given up trying, that we have Schubert but have become more or less brainless. No other country, I told Gambetti, has allowed the Catholic Church to rob it so unscrupulously of the faculty of thought, no other country has allowed itself to be decapitated, as it were, by Catholicism.

Lot of women in Western Civ. seem to have teamed up with a cat and a cello in lonely *ménages à trois*. This is not as straightforward a fate as you might imagine. You have to start learning a string instrument pretty EARLY. How do all those little girls have the prescience to realize they're going to end up alone and forgotten and in need of a huge human-shaped object to wedge between their legs? Do they know at *ten* they'll someday be plodding despondently through adulthood? Which comes *first*, the cat-cello combo or the emotional void (the cat and the cello might put some men *off*)?

Here I am in her country and not in her cunt. Maybe I should give Eloïse a call. But even if she REMEMBERS me she probably hasn't forgiven me. Women never seem to understand how easily one can fall into being a bastard, just by trying to do the Right Thing! All my sins of obfuscation, prevarication, procrastination, fornication. What a jerk I was. ABSOLVE ME, Eloïse!

All so long ago.

Nothing graceful in this gliding.
Blood and steam and sweat all BOUNCE off ice!
Mad and monstrous mix of elements:
Frozen water, noise and bustle,

Bluntly spat-out exclamations:
'Get 'im off me!' . . . 'Pass it to him!'
'Crazy goddam no-count bastard!'
So much instant ersatz hatred.

THIS, America was built on,
Hate is what my land is made of.
We are nothing but usurpers:
Mountains echo with our land-lust.
We, the burglars of peaceful nations –
Knifing chieftains bearing wampum!
Tribes condemned to gradual slaughter:
Smallpox did our killing for us.
Maya, Aztec, Inca, Mohawk,
Iroquois and Onondaga,
Cherokee and Cayuga:
Now they're names of CARS not death throes.

Archetypal 'Indian-giver',
I usurped, I faltered (flattered).
Gave my love and then retrieved it.
Rifled through her land of longing,
Left her with her reservations.

ELOÏSE

You want to fuck me? You want to? Fuck me with anything. Anything. Shove it in my mouth. Shove it down my throat. The sexual fever that wakes you from a dream of desperate masturbation, the search in the dream for some suitable object to appease the need, followed by the same search on waking. Needing a fuck, still in the dream of need, you stumble towards the bathroom, trying again – awake – to think of something that would serve the purpose. But nothing turns you on in that cold and silent bathroom. The shapes of the toothpaste tube, the moisturizer bottles, the ancient, slightly rusty hair-mousse canister, the dusty vitamin jars, even the dark blue rose-water bottle, are not it. You consider the possibility of a carrot but they're all in the fridge and probably too small and too cold and too old. The cucumber's gone soggy. Anyway, vegetables would require carving for maximum effect and that would take too long. There is in fact nothing to make up for the absence of a human prick at this moment, that is all you want, you want all that. A wank on the bathroom floor isn't it. But by now you're coming down, waking up, and a practical side has emerged, a consoling side that counsels patience, postponement, nothing to be done tonight, it'll have to wait till morning. You will have to find a mate, but in the morning. Or else a carrot. Until then the great urge will have to wait. You totter back to bed like a sleepwalker, beginning to feel horrified now by the sudden power of that need, the lust your sexless existence has so well hidden from you that it can only erupt when you're asleep. A huge impervious wave, with you its mermaid.

... a fertile female bee ...
is an egg machine.

On a scale of human suffering, Eloïse's six years' celibacy was of little account. But in an ideal world it would be recognized as the tragedy it was. This was a woman who from the age of *five* had suspected she wanted more sex than she would ever get.

There were days when she was alive to the sexiness of every tree trunk, days when her cunt protruded beyond its accustomed zone searching for its counterpart, days when all men seemed sweet.

Once, driving round a sharp bend on a hilly lane, she had to swerve to avoid a head-on collision with a white sports car. The other driver was smiling and for a moment Eloïse imagined his car accordioning into hers, flesh thwacked against flesh, the two of them fucking for a split second before they died. Died *happy*.

But in general she had no libido anymore. She had watched her mother die lost, her father die angry, her old cat in her arms die all unknowing. And she had endured another loss that was *like* a death. She had seen how the body can let you down, she had no faith in it. Her own was an empty shell through which ghosts of thoughts and desires occasionally wandered.

Worm shells, Ceriths, Sundials, Wentle-traps, Hairy shells, Cup-and-saucer limpets, Egg cowries, Necklace shells, Helmet shells, Frog shells, Fig shells, Strombs, Drupes.

Eloïse became obsessed with mangoes, their kindly glowing colours, bonny, fleshy blobs. To be surrounded by those colours! A return to the womb? At one stage in her solitude she put them on the window sills (twenty at a time!) and revelled, with secret creeping happiness, in these slowly softening spheres, each its own sunset, and in each a flat skeletal stone to gnaw on.

What happens if you have no hope? You slowly disintegrate. Eloïse got ailments to suit her current lifestyle: sizzled lips from sucking mangoes, heart pounding from sorrow and stagnation, nausea from eating standing up, piles from? sitting around?, spotty back from no hugging, atrophied cunt from no fucking, strange feeling in her throat from not speaking for days at a time, strained shoulders from dragging heavy things about, geriatric skin on her hands from having no good *use* for hands, and from too much washing. She washed her hands after going to the loo, before and after inserting tampons (toxic shock syndrome), before and after cooking, sometimes in between ingredients (*E. coli* bacteria), before and after eating, before and after washing up (during too, presumably), before and after writing a letter (clean paper; dirty ink), after unloading groceries, after taking out the rubbish, after shovelling coal or cat shit (toxoplasmosis), after feeding cats (salmonella), after handling smoke detectors (radioactive), after washing clothes, after hoovering, after being outside (tetanus).

When her hands became uncomfortably rough (snagging on tights and wool) she started rubbing moisturizers into them. But

36

moist hands attract dirt, thus leading to more washing. She was forever rubbing her hands with soap and oil, like a worried fishwife. It was one of the few sensual pleasures left to her – along with bending over the radio to marvel at the sounds human throats and tongues and lips can make, and walking in the wind. The wind encircled her, opened her coat, licked her tears.

She was like an old woman who expects nothing. No rights on the earth. Her main worry: that some day a male nipple under a taut shirt would so entrance her she'd make a grab for it before she knew what she was doing.

She got little crushes. She fell in love with her solicitor while he was handling her conveyancing (in fact she began to love him more than the *house* and was struck low when his secretary called instead of him to tell her the purchase was complete). Next it was the mover, whom she loved because he was careful with her stuff. Once she'd moved in, it was the gardener, not even *her* gardener but some *neighbour's* gardener, a man who was never happier than when wearing protective clothing and destroying something. Then it was a local architect, come to study her thatched roof. Each time, another load of lipstick wasted.

She fell so tumultuously in love with her moving-man that for a while she wondered if he was the love of her life! (She thought about him a good deal in her new bed in her new bedroom in her new house.) There was no obvious reason to love her moving-man except that he talked to her once in her dead parents' kitchen for hours in the gathering dusk. But this was enough.

He was in love with *moving*. He delighted in explaining the rudiments, followed by the finer intricacies, of moving. He spoke to her of three dimensions, the rightness of right angles, the squareness of the quintessential box – she made him repeat it all, just to listen to him talk. He tore at packing tape with his teeth like a lion, and demonstrated its strength by sticking some on his forearm, then ripping it off with a bold flourish. Oh, she didn't know what he was demonstrating, she was just looking at that forearm.

PSYCHOLOGICAL PHENOMENON OF FALLING IN LOVE WITH ONE'S MOVER ('TRANSFERENCE'):

Moving-man, meticulousness of; forearm of
Proper construction of a box
Rule that All Things Should Be In Boxes
Exceptions to rule that All Things Should Be In Boxes:

        a) hoover

        b) floor lamps

        c) paintings

        d) unwieldy house plants

        e) cats

        f) cello

        g) rugs

Packing procedure for dishes: upright
Scale of charges: a) with packing materials

                b) without

Legal redress in case of injury to:

        a) furniture

        b) mover

        c) movee

Tearing tape with teeth
Night he talked for hours in the darkening kitchen

Character of said conversation, purportedly about moving

His eyes ('not my best feature')

His sense of:　　a) honour

　　　　　　　　b) humour

　　　　　　　　c) three dimensions

He as the love of my life

Particulars of piano removal

His attitude to blocking neighbours' garage ('Fuck 'em!')

First mention of his wife

Arrangement for collection of collapsed cardboard boxes

She was alone, the days of her periods not noted, her successes and failures, her ailments, her longings, her leanings, her lists, her lethargy, her current *address*, the anniversary of her mother's death, likewise her father's, her birthdays, the years of her life passing unnoticed, unrecorded, life eddying by unseen. Everything that a man who loved her might have concerned himself with, *not noticed*.

This is what it's like to be an old woman. No wonder they give up the reproductive display.

GEORGE

Dumped out on the rowboat's prow,
She becomes a fish now, writhing,
And I mount her, in defiance
Of the Royal Edict, searching
For an opening, a cloaca –
Wondering if fish, like mermaids
Hide a hole amid their scales.

Round me in the waves swim naked
Children, bare as dolphins, choking
In the milk-green sea.

Each man to himself an I-land,
And on each a windswept longing
To be loved.

Of course my poem is all part of a self-inflicted and debilitating homesickness. I mourn. Lately it's taken the form of wanting to BAKE. I need to knead big white bulging buttocks of dough, need to *see* my braided chollah loaves, need to eat donuts made according to my father's secret recipe (he got out of night duty in the Navy with those donuts), need to chew my black molasses bread, and sugar cookies, star-shaped.

What I miss about my life then is the methodical nature of the baking process. Up at 4:00 to turn on the ovens and surround myself with warm rising mounds, my only worry: the age-old mysteries of yeast.

Now I lie on an English couch like an English drag queen doing a lousy Elizabeth Barrett Browning impression, grousing about English layabouts (usually whilst guzzling Famous Grouse). My own fecklessness disgusts me. My famous CONFUSION. Half the crimes of the Nazis were carried out through inaction, people doin' NUTTIN': I'm perfectly cut out for that job. Especially on a *Bank Holiday*. What a boring name that is. Why not Weltschmerz Day, National Malingerers' Day, Sexual Ambivalence Day, The Fucking Shops Are Shut Again Day?

I never made silly bread like walnut and tamarind brioches or pumpernickel pretzels. That stuff's for BORED bakers. Most exotic I ever got were the mango muffins I made for Eloïse. Useless muffled muffins.

> *Let me tell you of our story,*
> *Of the now and never will be,*
> *Of the sorrow and the changes:*
> *How I loved her, loved and left her.*

> *See me take her, turn her, learn her,*
> *See me take her hands and lead her*
> *To the bed we shared that night.*

> *Leave us there upon the bed now,*
> *Trembling, awkward, stunned, delighted.*
> *Silence all her protestations,*
> *All her mournful lamentations.*
> *Close the circle of her questions.*

I marvel at the life I once led: bread, wife, hockey practice twice a week, creative-writing classes to teach in Salem, Beverly, Danvers and Newburyport . . . and none of it enough to contain me. Had to fall in love as well (writing to Eloïse when I should have been finishing my POEM). And even so, I was still obliging Ivy once a week. Ivy, who cooked herself roast beefs in the middle of the night and left the basement sauna on for three months running once because her skunk of an ex-husband was paying the bills. She had spirit – until she hit sixty, had a boob job and went all practical on me. Learning to be an old lady, I guess.

I try to forget the bad things about the marriage, like my wife's Ten Commandments (pinned to the fridge by a heart-shaped magnet until I fell irretrievably from grace). I can only remember six of them now:

1 Fidelity (oh, god)
2 Tidiness
3 Romantic presents of flowers and candy
4 Share housework
5 Have children when SHE says so
6 Renew marriage vows once a year . . .

She's doing better than I am these days. Even her exaggerated DULLNESS seems essentially a good sign (of tranquillity, I guess). She's turned the bakery into a Down-Home-Spankin'-New-Eatin'-Tavern (actually I think she just calls it 'Lulu's'), all kitted out with red-and-white checked tablecloths, rag rugs, weird salads and low-priced watercolors by local artists. She makes her superb pecan pie along with two disgusting soups each day: Curried Clam

Chowder (yeccch!), Haddock Pineapple 'n' Lima Beans, Lobster 'n' Ginger, Shrimp 'n' Apple Dumpling, Lettuce ... When I expressed some disbelief that lettuce soup actually EXISTS, she sent me the recipe:

> Fry one onion until soft
> Add FOUR WHOLE LETTUCES (washed)
> 1 quart water
> Boil, purée, then add stock.

Me, PURÉE? Ten whole YEARS I spent with that woman! Ten whole lettuces.

She's now manifesting a mania for exercise, as jilted women so often do – though, come to think of it, she was always good at purposeless expenditures of energy. She doesn't seem to understand that joggers are the LIVING DEAD, loping their way straight toward a CORONARY. Who do they think they're kidding?

Now she's worried *I'm* going to pot because there's no ice hockey over here, only pinball. She holds up her friend Marge as an example of healthy living. 'Marge swam every day ...' Marge worked herself up into a terrifying peak of fitness, then swallowed a load of pills! MARGE KILLED HERSELF. Is this what she wants me to do? *Jeez*, why must I hear about Marge?

But at least she's TALKING to me these days. Not like near the end, when we seemed to sit on that bed for weeks silently surveying the ruins of our alliance. Now she's talking to EVERYONE and having a 'very stimulating year': goes to a printmakers' co-op, Spanish conversation class, walking club, quilting bee, reading group, drama group ... Might as well have

GROUP SEX while she's at it (probably does). Her and her stimulating year.

For a while I worried that SHE might commit suicide, didn't know WHAT she might do. My guilt was acute. But it turns out our divorce wasn't an event of cataclysmic proportions for her. I was just one among many men she might have married (might *yet* marry). Nothing special, plenty of fish in the sea. And yet I still feel guilty. Done that woman wrong ... Even Henry VIII must sometimes have barreled down those castle corridors shouting 'WHAT HAVE I DONE?'

Broodin' on the Boston Bruins
(Brave old team, now in ruins),
How they BUTCHERED their opponents
While in the stands the fans had punch-ups!
All a crime, a violation.
Not, as I thought, my salvation.
Not a metaphor for life, just
Strife.

Anger, coldness, hate and sorrow:
These men from each other borrow.
WOMEN's wishes, wombs and wisdom –
Wasted on wretches craving more
Familiar foes.

Lying on my English sofa, so
FAR from those old scenes of battle,
Rubbing the hockey stick we're born with.
All I know is that I loved her.
That I loved her, loved and left her.

ELOÏSE

Dear Sir or Madam,

I am writing to you because I am very concerned about my cats' present aversion to Whiskas cat food. I have had cats for over twenty-two years, and have been feeding them Whiskas cat food for at least eighteen of those years. Recently, however, they have become more and more choosy. They will now only accept the Select Cuts variety (and that not always), and reliably eat only the Select Menus which come in the half-size tins and are much more expensive when one has three cats.

Of the original type of Whiskas, they used to eat Lamb, Liver or Turkey flavours (after starting to refuse the Chicken, Rabbit and Beef). But now, even the stray cats outside won't eat the Turkey or Lamb recipes (which I left out for them when my own cats disdained them).

After all these years of depending on Whiskas to provide healthy and appetizing food, I am now having to explore other brands to try to find one my cats will tolerate. Have you done something to your recipes, your tins, or to my cats? I really cannot understand this radical change in their dietary preferences, and it is a great worry and inconvenience ...

Eloïse had reduced her contact with the outside world primarily to disputes with impersonal bodies. In the last year she had been in written communication with:

Whiskas

The Queen

Germaine Greer

Her old headmaster

John Lewis's

Oliver E. Prŷs-Jones

The DVLC

The RAF

The BBC

The police

Melvyn Bragg

Malcolm Rifkind

Two different accountants

Sainsbury's

Hoover plc

A tampon company

The Royal Mail

Two plumbers

Angus Deayton

A swimming pool

Her ex-flatmate, Howard

The doctor who killed her parents

A company that makes loo-roll holders

Margaret Thatcher

A cemetery

Carnation Evaporated Milk
The county council
Slumberland

She wrote to the Queen, Angus Deayton, Margaret Thatcher, Melvyn Bragg and Germaine Greer about their hatred of women. You can tell the Queen hates women by the way she greets the wives of foreign dignitaries. She simply isn't interested in them. She assumes they don't matter. Just because they're women, she assumes they have no power. 'This is not how bee societies work,' wrote Eloïse to the Queen. 'Not only do bees create an entire civilization from scratch every year, in which females are awarded due significance and respect, but they even have built-in *carrier bags* (pollen baskets) on their back legs.'

She asked Angus Deayton why there are so few women on his TV news quiz, and Melvyn Bragg why he always interrupts or ignores the women on his Monday-morning radio programme. To Germaine Greer she wrote, 'All you do these days is giggle and flirt. Your tautness has all unravelled (but perhaps we all come to that in the end)...'

Eloïse wrote to the council to claim her Single Person's rebate. She contacted the cemetery superintendent to inform him that someone had swiped a large rectangle of turf from her parents' joint grave (he had probably done it himself but she was trying to be tactful). She wrote to Slumberland to find out if they still made a particular type of mattress in a single-bed size (they didn't). She wrote to the BBC berating them for moving *Woman's Hour* from the morning to the afternoon or vice versa (whatever). She wrote to a tampon company about the way their boxes shower tampons all over the customer's knees when you open them. She wrote to one accountant for a breakdown of his £3,000 bill, and to another to engage his services because she was not going to pay the

£3,000 bill. She wrote to the RAF about Chinook helicopters flying within an inch of her roof on a daily basis, scaring her cats. She wrote to Malcolm Rifkind asking why he was doing nothing for the Bosnian Muslims. She wrote to the Minister for Roads about the foolishness of allowing men to drive cars. She wrote to the GP who killed her parents, accusing him of malicious conduct (her mother died from the strain of being given too many tests, her father killed himself because no one was effectively controlling his pain): 'He died without even saying goodbye. I have to *live* with this.' She wrote to her old headmaster, who had taught dancing: 'All the girls had to wait for a partner while the boys were allowed to dance *together* if they wanted to. The girls just had to sit there. If a boy was finally forced to dance with one of the girls, he'd pull his shirt cuffs down so our hands wouldn't touch, or just hold his hands up in the air out of reach.' She wrote to the judge who declared a raped eight-year-old girl 'no angel'. She wrote to the author of a book on bumblebees (Oliver E. Prŷs-Jones) about his instructions for amateur bee enthusiasts on how to kill bees. And she wrote to the local swimming pool: 'I was shocked and alarmed to find a large human turd floating in the water.' No reply.

> Dear Sir or Madam,
>
> If I'd wanted to live in Piccadilly Circus I could have stayed in London. I moved to the country for some peace and quiet. I had no idea that my house was on some daily helicopter flight-path.
>
> Is it absolutely necessary for them to fly so close? I often think they are actually going to crash into the house. This is terrifying, both for myself and my cats ...

In reply to an impertinent form-letter asking if she'd like to subscribe to some boring business magazine, Eloïse wrote:

You assume a lot about someone you've never even met. What makes you so sure I need to improve my leadership qualities?

I do not wish to know how Ikea makes money, nor do I believe that Nike shoes are expressive of emotion. *My* only 'company strategy' is to *avoid* company . . .

She wrote to her ex-flatmate about the couch:

Dear Howard,

In response to your recent letter, I have been thinking again about the couch. As I remember it, the couch was not in good condition when I first moved in. Its springs were sticking out in odd directions and it was very difficult to arrange the cushions comfortably. They never seemed to fit.

I was not overly concerned about this at the time, and regarded its gradual decay as an inevitable consequence of use, before and after my arrival. I honestly attributed the wonky arm to normal wear and tear.

I am also concerned that you were not satisfied with my efforts in the garden . . .

She had considered writing a letter that could be sent to all her former acquaintances –

GENERAL STATEMENT FOR ALL CONCERNED: I do not wish you to be perturbed in any way by my current uncommunicative behaviour. I wish it to be known that I am not pursuing any friendships at the moment because I cannot think of anything to say and I suspect I am bad for people. I am too egotistically involved with my own decay to focus on the troubles and triumphs of others . . .

– but managed to restrain herself. Instead she wrote an imaginary letter to herself from the outside world:

Dear Madam,

It has recently come to our attention here at the Inland Revenue that you are a bad girl, that you were bad to your parents and gradually, throughout the many years of your sorry existence, you have managed to alienate and/or injure everyone with whom you have come into contact, including animals and even inanimate objects.

Everyone in the world is sick of your moods, your incompetence, your car zooming this way and that, your droning radio, your total lack of courage and sexual plausibility.

Even your milkman is disgusted with you and will therefore no longer be supplying you with your daily lactose requirements. In fact he now feels such a repugnance towards you that the whole surrounding area will not be receiving milk either – for which your neighbours will no doubt blame you.

The entire matter has caused great shock and consternation in our office. We are therefore rescinding your annuity, your British citizenship, your human rights and any remaining connection you might mistakenly believe you have to the human race. You are no better than a bug.

She once bought four six-ounce tins of Carnation Evaporated Milk from Sainsbury's, mainly because they were offering a free Carnation Evaporated Milk tea towel if you sent in four labels. But when she got home she noticed that the offer had ended some months before. So she immediately despatched an irate letter to

Sainsbury's and a beseeching one to Carnation Evaporated Milk, begging them to send her a free tea towel anyway. Sainsbury's wrote back, offering her a refund if she returned all four tins (but she'd already used one). She never heard from Carnation Evaporated Milk.

Some time later, Eloïse received a mysterious parcel. Being wary of letter bombs, which had lately been in the news (women being particularly targeted), she quickly threw it into the garden. But, contemplating the package from her kitchen window, she realized it was her civic duty not to leave letter bombs lying about the garden, so she called the police. They told her to put the suspect package in the dustbin (as long as it wasn't a rubbish day) while they tried to trace its postmark.

Eloïse had forgotten all about the package when a policewoman rang back late that afternoon and left a message on the answering machine, confirming that it had come from a bona fide supply depot. Eloïse went out and retrieved the package, opened it, and found: a Carnation Evaporated Milk tea towel! Success.

> Dear Sir or Madam,
>
> I am returning to you the loo-roll holder I recently bought, as it does not fit into the holes it is meant to fit into.
>
> I was very excited at first to find it, as I had been looking for one for a long time, and the only others I have seen come in a pack containing the whole apparatus (i.e. not just the plastic cylinder that goes inside the loo roll but the attachment you're supposed to affix to the wall, which I do not need as in my loo there are already some ceramic tile supports to hold the loo-roll holder cylinder)...

> A helpful tip is not to breathe on bumblebees: cultivate the habit . . . of breathing from the side of your mouth when looking at them.

GEORGE

Position of ants in the Animal Kingdom ... Mode of observation ... Mode of marking ants – Stages in life of ants ... Length of life – Structure of ants ... Character of ants – Wars among ants – Modes of fighting – Soldiers ... Habitations of ants – Communities of ants Food – Enemies ... Games – Cleanliness ... Drowned ants Buried ants Instances of kindness – A crippled ant ... Behaviour to intoxicated friends ...

The creative-writing racket hasn't really hit England yet but I was able to get a writer-in-residence sinecure at London University this year, thereby enabling me to stay in the country a bit longer. All I have to do is go over there once or twice a week and encourage the poor slobs to write. Of course most of them need no encouragement – they need to SLOW DOWN. I'm pretty envious of their ideas. My envy makes me irascible. In fact I've scared off my best student.

At first she seemed to be getting a bit of a crush on me, which I don't LIKE but was calm about. Then she stopped coming altogether. Not only was she the brightest spark in a none-too-sparkly class, but she left all her WORK behind for me to read and I'd like to discuss it with her.

Last time I saw her was on the street one night after she'd just missed another of my classes. She was standing around outside a pub with some dopey-looking guys. I would have ignored her, but she called out to me, started telling me about some story she claimed to be writing, wanted to tell me all about it over the noise of the traffic. She probably meant this as some sort of atonement for missing the class, but I flipped.

'There you go,' I roared at her, 'just throwing your ideas away on some wet roadside! Either write it or *shut up* about it.'

CLOSE-UP OF GIRL'S SHOCKED EXPRESSION. SHOT OF WET ROADSIDE. SHOT OF THE DOPEY GUYS DISCONSOLATELY SHUFFLING THEIR FEET.

CLOSE-UP OF COBBLESTONES BEING SPATTERED WITH MUD AS CARS ZIP BY.

Haven't seen her since. What a jerk – and now I'm stuck with her NOTEBOOK.

One of her stories is about an erect penis that runs amok in a crowd of Saturday shoppers, then seeks sanctuary in a dank, dark cellar where it meets a lot of other erect penises, makes some good lifelong pals (erect penises turn out to have a much less competitive streak than you might think!), and together they set off for a faraway land where they won't get arrested anymore and can be themselves, out in the open. They roll, bounce, limp and burrow their way to a better life.

She was wasted on those dopey guys.

One of my more annoying students is pursuing me at the moment. Venetia. I'm always getting commandeered by older women, not necessarily for sex but as some kind of *lapdog*. Or some kind of *FREAK*: American poet with hang-up about ice hockey in need of?? Smothering, evidently. She's a restaurant critic, hugely wealthy, totally talentless, but nonetheless a self-proclaimed *darling* of the English literary scene (bunch of snails sniffing each other's snail trail). Writers turn her on. She's always on her way to or from the memorial service of some supposedly noteworthy literary type. Just LOVES a good funeral.

The rest of the time, she can be found in Ian McEwan's favorite restaurant hoping to catch sight of him or one of his pals (she'd stalk SALMAN RUSHDIE if she could only FIND him). Failing these, she'll settle for any sonuvabitch who can hold a pen. Hence, *moi*. I am her current PROJECT, god help me. She thinks I live too isolated a life, wants to introduce me to all her dull bookish friends. She does this by making us eat her FOOD.

This isn't ENGLISH cuisine, it's weirder than that. She'll go all the way over to France for the weekend just to buy BOUDIN SAUSAGES: deathly WHITE in color and tasting of urine. Or she'll come back from Indonesia and insist on plopping a RAW EGG in your soup – in a country rife with salmonella! She once presented me with a long gray slab of HALF-COOKED WHOLEMEAL (aaagh!) PASTRY dotted with wrinkled cherry tomatoes and soiled with bits of charred oregano: 'Pizza'. Another time, she MICROWAVED a CAKE: mixed it for 30 secs, microwaved it for 10, tested it (not done), microwaved it for another 2½ secs and SERVED it. I managed to forgo. But I'd finally figured out the mystery of all those funerals: she's gradually poisoning the whole literary establishment!

When not cooking she's truffle-hunting for gossip. She LOVES my divorce. Grilled me on it with such vehemence and vengeance one night, such relentless insensitivity (forget English tact, just

FORGET it), that I don't expect ever to *forgive* her. She sees my wife as some sort of long-suffering, middle-class, bottle-recycling Laura Ingalls Wilder, left behind in the doorway of a cute log cabin dripping with maple syrup . . . And I'm the rogue. This pleases Venetia.

She doesn't realize my roguish days are over. The last woman I slept with brushed her TEETH all the time. I felt I must brush mine an equivalent amount. Now I associate sex with spearmint.

> My dear lady, this is a list
> Of the beauties my master has loved,
> A list which I have compiled.
> Observe, read along with me.
> In Italy, six hundred and forty;
> In Germany, two hundred and thirty-one;
> A hundred in France; in Turkey ninety-one.
> In Spain already one thousand and three.
> Among these are peasant girls,
> Maidservants, city girls,
> Countesses, baronesses,
> Marchionesses, princesses,
> Women of every rank,
> Every shape, every age.

Honouring the memory of the esteemed personage who died mysteriously the other day after eating a raw egg in his soup were:

> Earl Lloyd George of Dwyfor, Lord and Lady
> Kilmarnock, the Hon Gerard Noel, the Hon
> Emma Soames, Mr Ferdinand Mount, Sir
> Mervyn and Lady Brown, Sir Frank Kermode,

Sir Kenneth Bradshaw, Mr John Bayley and Dame Iris Murdoch.

Mr Anthony Howard, *The Times*, Mrs Katie Campbell, *Evening Standard*, Mrs Jane Mays, *Daily Mail*, Mr Mark Le Fanu, General Secretary, Society of Authors, Mr Eddie Bell, Executive Chairman and Publisher, HarperCollins, Ms Gail Rebuck, Random House UK, Mr Peter Carson, Penguin Books, Mr Peter Janson-Smith, Chairman, Glidrose Publications, Mr Bruce Hunter, David Higham Associates, Mr Denis Doble, Consul-General for Amsterdam.

Mr Anthony Butcher, QC, Chairman, Garrick Club, and Mrs Butcher, with Mr Martin Harvey, Secretary; Mr John Heald, the Betjeman Society, and Mrs Heald, Mrs Lisa Parkes, Walton Theatre Collection, Mrs Yvonne Simmons, St Anne's College, Oxford, Mr Ian Hall, Chairman, Bloomsbury Society for Racial Harmony in the Arts, Mr Eric Shorter, Director, The Royal Theatrical Fund.

Mr Peter Taylor, Mr David Plante, Mr Norman Garrod, Mr and Mrs Tom Maschler, Mr Bernard Levin, Prof and Mrs John Postgate, Mr and Mrs Anthony Thwaite, Mr Alan Brien, Mr D. H. Enright, Mr Christopher Horne, Mrs Jill Day-Lewis, Mr Geoffrey Moore, Dr Patricia Gillam, Mr David Williams, Mrs James Gibb, Miss Emma Gibb, Mrs Colin Welch, Mr Dermott Clinch, Mr Patrick Garland, Mr Alan Ross, Mr Paul Levy, Mr William Boyd, Mr Paul Johnson, Mr Paul Sidey, Mr and Mrs Richard Hough, Ms Miriam Gross, Mr Derek Nimmo, Mr Alan Jenkins, Mr Alan Watkins, Miss Isabel Fonseca.

Mrs Robin Orr, Ms Wendy Cope, Ms Antonia Phillips, Miss Livia Gollancz, Mr Nick Rankin and Dr Maggie Gee, Mr Salman Rushdie, Ms Rosie Boycott, Mr Lionel Bloch, Mr Keith Waterhouse, Mr Paul Ferris, Mr Donald Trelford and many other friends.

THE SEXUALLY FRUSTRATED WOMAN

Like a newly released convict, the sexually frustrated woman is predisposed to passion and on the prowl. She supposes herself *ripe*, and she is *everywhere*. Hear her giggling? Feel the tension when you sit beside her on the bus or innocently obtrude your knee between hers on the Tube?

Study her life history and you will find that despite some quite promising early years she has retreated increasingly into herself. By obsessively substituting food, booze, embroidery and the banging of pots and pans for sex she has become an Autonomous Rogue Female. Every few months she will send off an airmail letter to some long-lost love object who rarely if ever replies. She is a nervous fretful companion with nothing to say for herself, prone to hysterical outbursts and the sudden poignant disclosure of irrelevancies. For a social life she relies heavily on the radio.

Her hormones are leaping, her heart is leaping, the *woman* is leaping (when not weeping). Avoid this demon. Try to mistake her for an inanimate object. Lower your eyes in her presence: eye contact is provocative. Do not speak to her if you can help it – her passions are easily aroused. Even a 'hello' or 'excuse me' could be misinterpreted. Tone down your costume, do not dress up when out in public – you could be accused later of having 'asked for it'. It is unsavoury to meet a sexually voracious woman down a dark alley so keep to main streets and well-lit areas. In fact, if you're a sexually unavailable man, why not just stay home? For your every courtesy is a cruelty. Look at the pain you cause when incautious of where you direct your stares, your winks, your smiles, your D.I.Y. advice. You leave a trail of devastation, a bunch of tantalized women who may never forget you, may base all hopes and preferences on the formative experience of having met you, and may berate their present and future partners for not being you. Bear this in mind when next you try to interest some strange woman in the falling pound. This woman is alert to every touch, even that of a fly, a raindrop, a car's *gear-stick*. Try not to be friendly or good-looking. You are dealing with ungovernable lust and there are certain responsibilities involved.

(from the absent student's notebook)

> *Denver, Dekalb, Garson, Gary –*
> *Chippewa, Saskatchewan.*
> *Colonizer – colonized.*
> *Man and woman, yeastlike mystery:*
> *Love and sadness rise there swiftly,*
> *Kneaded (NEEDED) into being.*
> *Flesh is both our doom and our delight.*

ELOÏSE

One day ant and bee flew
out to do some shopping.
Bee told ant they must not
buy too much or the basket
would get too heavy.
Now ant and bee are flying home.
Doesn't the basket look full!
The basket is too heavy!!!!

(Would you like to know what is in the basket? I'll tell you.)

1 little LETTUCE

2 little TARTS

3 little BANANAS

4 little CAKES

5 little APPLES

6 little EGGS

7 little BISCUITS

8 little SAUSAGES

9 little CARROTS

10 little GRAPES

(Isn't it a lot! No wonder the basket is too heavy!)

My tragedy doesn't strike anyone else as a tragedy, my poignant sorrow moves no one. I regret everything I have ever done and everything that has ever happened to me. Death is all around me. This does not make you strong. I am frightened of the whole world and its hostility to me.

My neighbours are my true oppressors, them and their skinny, stripy, naked-looking dog like a penis on wheels, and their bratty little boy who's always trying to destroy his own toys, and their clapped-out Mercedes-Benz. Our cottages are semi-attached to each other in such a way that when they go up and down their stairs, it sounds like they're on *mine*. And they never walk, it's always a gallop. When not galloping they're persecuting the kid. I once heard the mother yell at him, 'Nobody likes you!', which is probably true but not kind. I thought about reporting them to Social Services but they'd know it was me, and anyway, I didn't come all the way out here to save the world (only to save myself).

The father's German, hence his devotion to the Mercedes, which he keeps in a state of total collapse right outside my kitchen window. He's forever tinkering with it, blowing his noxious fumes at me for hours at a time. Nazis.

They had a burglary. Banged on my door to ask if I'd seen a green and white van outside on the day. Did I move here to study traffic? (Actually I hardly ever look out of my front windows in case some bloody villager is looking *in*.) Then the wife decided that, as her husband and I are usually about during the day, we should let each other know when we're going out so that we can mutually guard each other's house. Did I give up all of human society in order to report my every movement to a Nazi who thumps up and down stairs all day, yells at his son and incessantly fixes his car? (He *whistles* too.) To sum up, am I to change my entire way of life because *they* got their hi-fi stolen?

60

I can't even go to the loo in peace anymore. Knock-knock at the door. When I arise and go to it (noting on the way that a goldfish has died) I find the husband across the lane shuffling about in the garage, as is his wont. I apologize for taking so long to come to the door. He requests an electric drill. I have already informed the wife that I don't stock any useful electrical devices but he clearly does not believe this. He can see no point in my *existence* – weird ageing solitary female – unless I can provide equipment of benefit to my neighbours. I am meant to feel guilty because I cannot help him with his drill needs. Now he'll have to go into town specially, so that he can install his burglar-proof window locks. How to convey to him that I don't give a shit?

Back to the loo to put a suppository up my bum. They're the same shape as atomic missiles and have roughly the same effect. Only a hermit could get away with it. 'Nobody likes you.'

Why'd the fish die?

> Dissection of a queen caught seeking a hibernation site reveals a massive clear or white fat body that may occupy most of the abdominal cavity … in spring the fat body is almost exhausted.

Why enquire, why amass knowledge? Why this widely held notion that we should be improving ourselves all the time? Cats aren't trying to improve. Sheep don't improve. Why send teenagers with terminal illnesses to school? It only makes sense if you believe in reincarnation and think you need to graduate *up* in the next life.

Someone is making a terrible racket outside with a lawnmower.

Spring! A pitiless revenge is being wreaked against nature with the aid of electricity. The countryside is just one big battleground. Did I come here to listen to that whining? Hard to tell where it's coming from. I now think it may be a hedge trimmer – I can hear the sound of tiny branches being wrenched untimely from their parent stalks. Gardening is obscene. If I went out now I'd probably be *beheaded*. I'm a prisoner in my own home. Alone, unloved, unprotected, lacking counsel of any kind.

One of my cats reminds me of my mother. I pat my mother in her. Reincarnation of evaporated mother.

How to stop missing her?

Born alone, live alone, die alone

> There is a strange duality of character in the bee. In the heart of the hive all help and love each other. They are as united as the good thoughts that dwell in the same soul. Wound one of them, and a thousand will sacrifice themselves to avenge its injury. But outside the hive they no longer recognise each other. Mutilate them, crush them -- or rather, do nothing of the kind; it would be a useless cruelty, for the fact is established beyond any doubt -- but were you to mutilate, or crush, on a piece of comb placed a few steps from their dwelling, twenty or thirty bees that have all issued from the same hive, those you have left untouched will not even turn their heads. With their tongue ... they will tranquilly continue to absorb the liquid they hold more precious than life, heedless of the agony whose last gestures are almost touching them, of the cries of distress that arise all around ... they have not the slightest sense of solidarity or pity.

GEORGE

'He *has* got *lovely hands*, this man' – British tennis commentator (MALE).

June. Classes over for the year. Screenplay in the clammy palms of Charles at the BBC. All I have to do now is finish me pome. Hence: TORPOR in front of the TV, watching Wimbledon. It's mayhem this year though, because there are some BRITISH players for once. Sort of interesting really – who'd have thought the British could be so belligerent? They are unreservedly, unrestrainedly nationalistic. They're all REDNECKS under the skin, sustained by strawberries 'n' cream. Their patriotism has been allowed to run RAMPANT. (Never had a Vietnam War to give them some SHAME.)

All they care about is BRITAIN and, now, BRITISH TENNIS. The fact that none of their players has ever won a match worth winning doesn't seem to stop the baying crowd thinking they *might*. If everybody YELLS loud enough. No feelings are spared for the unfortunate opponent (they cheer his every blunder). But that's English POLITENESS for ya. Their xenophobia's completely out of hand. It's narcissism really, and it's SCARY. And if they're like this when their man's obviously losing, what would they be like TRIUMPHANT? Lynch mobs? CONCENTRATION CAMPS?

Can't help thinking that most of Benjamin Britten's (enormous) reputation here's due to his name being BRITTEN. They just LAP that kind of thing up. Their famous tolerance is a *farce*. They hate EVERYBODY – they just get away with it by hating us all *equally*. The latest news flash is that anti-Semitism is on the decline here. Like hell it is!

They treat the Irish like shit too:

> Irish people in Britain suffer discrimination at work, are dismissed as scroungers by DSS staff, are bullied by their neighbours and are targeted by police ... Harassment at work includes name-calling and Irish jokes, which 79 per cent of people surveyed said they found offensive. Many said they were "deeply wounded" when colleagues automatically assumed they had sympathy for the IRA.

How do they get away with it?! Try telling one of those Irish jokes in a Boston bar! Fuckers.

I'm beginning to think Venetia's after my BODY after all. Her behavior's increasingly peculiar. She admires a shirt I'm wearing. Next week, SHE'S wearing it (or something very similar). She's read up on ICE HOCKEY and quizzes me on the finer points. I used to be able to get *rid* of people by blasting 'em with ice hockey trivia! Not Venetia. Now she's bought herself a cappuccino machine, in imitation of the one I got for judging a short-story competition (poor recompense) – but of course *she* has to get one that WORKS.

Yes, everything she has is slightly BETTER than my version. It's copycat stuff with a resentful twist to it. She doesn't just want to climb all over me, she wants to SUPERCEDE me in some way. It's not friendly. She goes and buys something because *I* have it, buys it without asking me if it's worth having, then BLAMES me when she finds out it isn't. Jesus, I am becoming responsible for her WHOLE LIFE and I hardly KNOW the woman!

She made me come with her to a DIRK BOGARDE READING the other night, reluctance issuing from every pore of my being. He wasn't too bad in the end. But even Dirk Bogarde and his exhaustive memories of infancy couldn't make up for the fact that I was worried the whole time that Venetia was about to slip her hand into my PANTS. The woman gives me the *creeps*.

Earlier this spring I made the mistake of admitting to Venetia that I was looking for a writing studio in which to finish my poem – somewhere separate from *home* and *bed* and the *kitchen* and this damn *couch* I seem to like so much – and she offered me her – get this! – MOVABLE GAZEBO, in the backyard of her vast property on Primrose Hill. You can MOVE IT AROUND so that it CATCHES THE SUN. Pretty irresistible. So I install my typewriter, my pens, my pencils, my MAGIC MARKERS, my paper, my stapler, my erasers, my paper clips, my Scotch tape, my scissors, my Boston Bruins calendar, stamps, envelopes, postcards, dictionary, thesaurus, other people's poems, my coffee thermos, RUG for my FEET, tapes, tape player, cushion, some socks, spare sweater, desk lamp, suntan lotion and what exists of my poem; and I settle down, planning to start off by writing something about writing something about writing something until I disappear neatly up my own littry ass ... All on the understanding that this corny but adorable little den is all MINE for the time being, PRIVATE, no INTRUDERS, no GLANCING AT STUFF left lying around in manuscript form, no admission AT ALL in fact when I'm not there, no nonsense, no NOTHIN'.

Then – exotic flowers start turning up. On my desk. In exquisite little vases. A black *lily* from Guatemala or some other strange sprig. The occasional snack would also appear out of nowhere. Only a matter of time before she'd be bringing me my SLIPPERS and PIPE!…

Had to cancel the whole arrangement, move my stuff OUT. (Gazebo-less in Gaza!) Venetia became very *cool* after that, which was alarming, but basically satisfactory. But soon she was back in action, calling me up for coffee. I felt I must *go* (out of guilt), and there she was, using my THERMOS. Or an exact imitation!

I hide at home with my very private thoughts about Eloïse. I want her so much it makes me cry.

ELOÏSELOÏSELOÏSELOÏSELOÏSELOÏSELOÏSELOÏSELOÏSE

Pros	*Cons*
her skin	cold feet
her lovely eyes	(kind of BIG feet too)
her wrists	too much lipstick (wrong color?)
HER	English
we're in same country	RESERVED
SHE LOVED ME	worrier (hypochondriac?)
her hand on my thigh	awkward, kind of clumsy
my cock down her throat	MAD at me?

66

cats

probably wants KIDS

bit iffy about ice hockey

long-lost, gone

long-gone, LOST

too late, TOO LATE

STAR-CROSSED LOVERS

They were made for each other. They both liked ice cream, fossils, ping-pong and opera. Both were moderate drinkers and non-smokers. Both were on the lookout for a long-term commitment.

Unfortunately they lived on separate planets and, through the incompetence of astronomers who assumed that her planet's cumulus clouds were icebergs, and the pigheadedness of bureaucrats and politicians who refused to allocate adequate funds for space exploration, the two potential love-birds were destined never to meet. Plans to colonise her planet were put on hold for another 300 years, by which time he was dead and she could barely hobble out to have a look at the alien spacecraft.

Thus, all chance of romance was knocked firmly on the head.

(from the absent student's notebook)

ELOÏSE

Eloïse's list of daily achievements:

Monday

1 Hoovered.
2 Tidied kitchen.
3 Cooked chicken, prepared vegetables.
4 Decided to write down things I accomplish every day because I never feel I've accomplished anything.
5 Washed hair.

Tuesday

1 Took bottles to bottle bank.
2 Shopped; unloaded shopping from car; put shopping away in cupboards.
3 Cleaned up kitchen.
4 Skimmed accountant's letter.

Wednesday

1 Paid milk bill.
2 Made vet appointment.
3 Bought TV guide.
4 Made big supper. *Too* big; froze some.

Thursday

1 Washed two loads of clothes.

2 Took cat to vet.

3 Read George's old letters in order to throw away; kept them.

4 Read accountant's letter in full.

Friday

1 Made bed (wished I could get back in).

2 Washed hair.

3 Had flat tyre; got it fixed.

4 Cured headache with paracetamol.

Eloïse wept easily these days. She was about to have a good cry in the car one day when she got a flat tyre. Hoping she could manage not to cry in public, she duly delivered herself and car to the tyre-repair place, got the tyre fixed at small financial expense but considerable of *time* (while she waited in the rain which was falling horizontally), then took off home. Blessed relief of being alone and homeward-bound. *Considered* weeping. But halfway home, the same tyre went exceptionally suddenly flat again. Eloïse had to change the wheel herself on a desolate country lane, kicking things a lot, feeling irate and swindled and preparing a tirade. 'I could have been *killed,*' she wanted to say, but she knew nobody cared at the tyre-repair place whether she was alive or dead. So in the end all she said was, 'I'm very annoyed.' Got a free tyre anyway. (Success!) While they put it on, she waited in the waiting room, undone by anger and her own bold words. She wondered if she might cry *then* but was determined not to make a spectacle of herself, there being a spectacle in the waiting room already of a different sort: a young woman wearing leather trousers. Eloïse sat in disgrace, wet ringleting hair and no leather anywhere, trying to stop shaking.

Eloïse had learnt to talk to men of nothing. She even wore her mother's engagement ring on her old-lady hand so that men would not feel cruelly compelled to mention their wives and girlfriends as soon as they saw her.

So she was appalled when a man winked at her at an auction (she was still looking for bits and pieces of furniture for her cottage). Auctions are usually perfectly good places for hermits. The only eye contact necessary is with the auctioneer, and then only briefly. A hermit can spend a whole day in catatonic stupor at an auction.

So this wink alarmed her. She smiled valiantly, trying to seem adult (?) but crumpled inwardly. She was in such a state of inner torment in fact that she could not look in the man's direction again for *two hours*, by which time she'd forgotten what he even looked like – but still feared him. All she knew was that if he winked at her again she might let out some strange cry and/or blush, and/or weep. To cope, she had to convince herself that it had not been a wink at *her* but perhaps some sort of secret signal to an auction ally *behind* her. Sufficiently calmed by this assumption to make a bid of her own, she managed to acquire an old shabby mirror in which to look at her shabby old self. No bargain.

Then she was off to the music shop, which she'd never visited before and had been nerving herself to enter for some weeks. She had heard Weber's Clarinet Quintet, or one movement of it at least, on Classic FM and was determined to hear it again (she was at war with *silence)*. But the shop was too quiet, manned by a seedy bloke sitting behind a desk. She felt like she had intruded on his *home* – he looked as if he ate and slept in that chair.

He seemed to find her request for a tape of Weber's Clarinet Quintet odd. But she was used to everything she uttered sounding strange to people, and smiled gamely.

'Cassette tapes aren't that easy to get hold of these days,' he muttered.

'Oh, yes, I know,' she gabbled. 'I haven't caught up with the modern era . . .'

He looked at her piercingly. 'You ought to come upstairs sometime.' Then, catching her startled expression, he added hastily, 'To see our collection of CD players.'

Awful purple-faced struggle to leave her name and phone number after this. She couldn't have cared less about Weber any more. Best *never to leave the house.*

> Poor ant was hurt,
> so bee said they would
> live in the house till
> ant got better.
>
> Bee put ant to bed
> to get better.

Eloïse took her antique clock to the jeweller's shop to be repaired: it could neither tick nor chime. The clock-man took it off to the back room but would not give Eloïse a receipt. That was Not How They Did Things There.

Eloïse thought she could handle this but later succumbed to terrible suspicions, nervous episodes, bad dreams. *How dare he take my clock? My father gave me that clock!. . .*

Distraught but defiant, she finally decided to go back to the shop to see how her clock was doing. She searched the clock-man's face   ·

for devious intent while she made polite enquiries after the clock (at least the man was *there*, and not heading for the nearest port with an irregularly chiming bundle under his arm).

The clock-man went to the back room and returned with a huge chunk of inner workings (supposedly from Eloïse's father's clock), called the 'movement'. He then embarked on a lengthy explanation of horological technology that involved a spring breaking, a cylinder warping, bulging and/or cracking, and all in all a tedious conglomeration of metal machinery reaching a sickening and unedifying standstill: the 'movement' no longer *moved*. All due to a terrible shock, a sudden change of temperature at some point in the past. Then Eloïse remembered dutifully putting the clock up in the freezing loft for a while after the neighbours' burglary. She thought she could hear the *boing!!!* now of clock springs unravelling in that sad and silent loft . . .

The clock-man asked her for £10 towards the expensive repairs he deemed necessary. But at least she got a *receipt* for the £10.

Yet she continued to dream of clocks, treachery, and undeserved kindnesses: a cheap imitation of her clock arrives in the post. She storms into the shop to complain about being palmed off with the *wrong clock*. The clock-man (now surprisingly handsome) explains that she's been sent a temporary replacement as a special honour for valued customers, while her clock is being fixed. Backing away shamefaced, Eloïse starts to apologize, but the clock-man then expresses great interest in her clock *fixation*. He asks gently if it's anything to do with mortality, or perhaps her *biological clock*. . . Now in *love* with the clock-man, Eloïse replies, 'No . . . I just thought I was being swindled.' End of dream.

Eloïse still half-believed all the men in the world were after her worldly possessions.

OWEN

Owen dreamed he was being shown around a marine research station, far out to sea. At first the vessel – a hollow cylinder – seemed immobile, though it was being beaten by twenty-foot waves which Owen could easily see through a huge window. Turning, he found the same was happening on the other side, except the waves here seemed if anything fiercer. You could look right into them: they were wild, frenzied, no-man-fathomed, green near the edges, darker inside, and so deep. When they got worse, the cylinder began to rock freely, riding the waves by rolling over on to its side, back upright, then over the other way. Owen was just supposed to *endure* this!

Ellen was always on the lookout for a better name than 'Ellen'. She felt her parents had belittled her, had branded her as ordinary, with this dull name (though they had only wanted to give her the roof-over-your-head a familiar name provides). She was forever coming up with new names for herself: Sally one day, Stephanie the next, Sophie, Anastasia, Sarah, Libuska, Myfanwy… Romilly… Some rotated and returned to live another day, long after Owen thought she'd finished with them.

On the way to the auction to purchase a desk for her (if possible), Ellen asked suddenly, 'Why didn't you call me Persephone?'

As soon as she said it, Owen began to wonder the same thing – Persephone was the perfect name for Ellen. Why *hadn't* they thought of it? Names are awarded with such needless haste before you have any idea of the person you're dealing with.

'I hereby rename you Persephone,' he offered lamely.

Ellen shook her head, even crosser now. 'That won't work! Nobody else is going to call me Persephone.'

'They'll catch on.'

'No, they won't. It's too late.'

The bus trundled on, Owen grimly hopeless, Ellen hopeful but grim.

Owen's wife had been reading *Moby Dick* while pregnant, an ocean inside her. She was determined to finish the book before giving birth. It took her six months! Finally, the battered paperback on its shelf, waters broke, and a baby with eyes like a whale's beached itself on the bed: Ellen.

You know how women are always jumping off piers to save their dogs? A Jack Russell or Yorkshire terrier or some other unsea-worthy canine creature is swept off a slippery promenade by a freak wave and in her distress and pity the mistress pops right in after it not knowing until she hits the water that her muscles will immediately become numb in the cold and she will have difficulty keeping her head above the swell and the mammoth weight of the water will edge her rhythmically towards the slimy ballasts of the pier and she won't even be able to see the dog now that she's level with it. This is reported briefly in the next day's papers.

It wasn't that their dog wasn't worth saving, a gentle fellow who never barked. Of course she couldn't just watch him drown. At first, though worried, Owen had yelled encouragement from the pier. He recognized that it was inconvenient to get your clothes wet on a Sunday stroll, but she would save the dog and they would hurry home, get a taxi perhaps if they could find one. He would make her a cup of tea with lots of sugar in it and drag blankets down from upstairs to wrap her in. He could even see the steaming cup of tea in his mind, a nice shiny red cup on a red saucer, like a cup of tea from an advert. In fact, it *was* a cup of tea from an advert – they had no red cups and saucers at home! Later, when the fakeness of this image came back to him, he realized he must already have given up hope. But at the time he didn't know that.

Minutes passed and neither she nor the dog had emerged from under the pier. Hypothermia, he thought. They might have to go to the hospital, just to have her checked out. Holding Ellen to his chest, he ran screaming back towards the shore, begging for help, trying not to trip over on the wet uneven planks. But he no longer remembers this. All he remembers is standing there staring at his wife's head as she bobbed out of sight under him. It seems to him he did nothing (though what he did was hold Ellen); the memory is frozen at the point when he stood there paralysed, purposeless.

He sometimes wonders now what Ellen must have thought, so silent in his arms. Does she think this is what you do when some-one you love is drowning, just *stand* there?

WHAT ELLEN THOUGHT: She remembers the scene (or thinks she does) from afar. A man and a girl (she doesn't know she was a baby) stand motionless as a woman sinks into the sea. She doesn't remem-ber her father running, or the people trying to help, the empty life-ring, her father's sobs. She's fallen for his version of events. She only remembers them standing there.

And she thinks they should have done something, not just let her mother go, not just watch her die.

ELOÏSE

Dear Madam,

I have been informed by my client that there seem to be at least three cats on your premises.

Unfortunately, they are also frequently to be found on or near my client's property. My client has more than once had the unpleasant experience of coming upon rodent remains. He has found a mouse's large intestine or duodenum leaking juices into his doormat. This same doormat has also on one occasion been soiled by feline faeces to a diameter significantly greater than that of the deposit itself.

May I inform you that neighbouring gardens are not to be used as an open sewer? Excretions of pets and/or their owners are not to be left on common or neighbouring property.

Yes, my cats shat on the mat. I hate my cats, but I hate the neighbours more. The wife had the cheek once to tell me I don't look Jewish; people always seem to think this is a *compliment*.

I started to apologize to her about the cats, but all that came out were the sordid unbearable details of my mother's death! To the neighbour's obvious alarm – *my* guts on her paving stones . . .

But not to worry. The wound clotted. I shan't be bleeding all over her again.

I care about no one.

Are all its leaves needle-like?
Do the needles grow singly?
Is the bark soft and spongey?
Does it have an undivided trunk?
Is its fruit berry-like?
Are the cones more or less spherical?

OK, I admit it. I killed my parents. Oh, their GP pitilessly mishandled them, in (curiously) opposite ways: over-zealous with my mother, who only needed to be left alone; stubbornly unmoved by my father, who only needed painkillers. But I *killed* them, I stood by and watched them decay and did nothing. Watched, while the doctors tinkered with my mother's body until she could take no more – no more *doctors* – and died in order to escape them. Watched as my father drifted into an impenetrable despair. Watched as he took his Nurofen!

I failed them.

How sharper than a serpent's tooth it is
To have a thankless child!

He must have been very angry to leave me like that, without a word. But even my father would not have stayed angry for six years! When I think of that, the guilt lilts a little, this heavy bag of guilt I take with me everywhere. He would not still be angry.

Maybe his suicide had nothing to do with me, maybe it was a wholly personal matter, a final declaration of loathing for the *world*, not me? A world in which life begins and ends in a hospital full of strangers. Born alone, live alone, die alone. Maybe it was a private matter and I have no right to intrude. Let him have his death. But a daughter *should* intrude on her father's death, it is not too much to ask. Instead, I left him to his despair. I have to live with this.

Driving me to the station once, my father had a minor collision with a bus. The bus driver jumped out, full of needless fury, spluttering, 'All incidents must be reported', and accused my father of being drunk. My father was *dying*. He was not drunk.

Are the leaves thick and fleshy?
Are the leaves regularly toothed?
Are the leaves hairy?
Are the lobes rounded?
Is it weeping?

OWEN

Consider the subtleness of the sea; how its most dreaded creatures glide under water, unapparent for the most part, and treacherously hidden beneath the loveliest tints of azure ... Consider ... the universal cannibalism of the sea ...

Consider all this; and then turn to this green, gentle, and most docile earth; consider them both, the sea and the land; and do you not find a strange analogy to something in yourself? For as this appalling ocean surrounds the verdant land, so in the soul of man there lies one insular Tahiti, full of peace and joy, but encompassed by all the horrors of the half known life.

WHAT ELLEN LIKES: Monopoly, Pound Puppies, card games, Cluedo, Chinese food, Pepperami sausages, Start cereal, Barbie dolls, noodles, some pop music, Nancy Drew books, Hitchcock movies, US sitcoms, women's magazines, horse-riding, a hall light on at night, stability, an electric blanket, all animals.

WHAT ELLEN DISLIKES: her name, sharks, snails, slugs, moths, earwigs (in fact all bugs), dentists, doctors, know-it-alls, scolders, earache, *Jane Eyre, Lord of the Flies, White Fang*, fox-hunting, her mother's death, injustice.

WHAT ELLEN HAS: one parent, willpower, tangled hair, teeth (both baby and adult), a diary, a taste for drawing complex rabbit warrens, a baby blanket her mother knitted her, a room full of animal toys (hard and soft), a fear of mortality, alien abduction and burglars, an unappeasable sadness.

All animals lick themselves with love. It's natural. Owen wished he loved his life a little bit, like a cat who licks herself, imagining life to be worth the effort of upkeep. The cat thinks so.

He'd finally exploded with Ellen. Her illnesses always threw him. He dreaded them. He'd once overheard a mother say that she loved her children most when they were ill, but he found Ellen's illnesses a provocation. They frequently brought him to the brink of disaster.

She had been ill in bed for two days when he finally tore round the room accusing her of messiness, illness, selfishness. He even railed against her choice of friends (there was one little boy he particularly disliked, who didn't say 'please' and was always asking what time it was). A pathetic scene: healthy man versus small sick girl. Ellen lay there, resigned to her fate, bracing herself against the onslaught, trying not to aggravate him further but none the less flinching irritatingly sometimes when he said something particularly hurtful. The flinching and, underneath it, her resilience, only make him want to yell at her more, to *break* her.

It scares him. He has to lock himself in the bathroom for fear of encircling her throat with his hands. He longs to kill them both, feels they would both benefit from it! Almost feels he *has* to do it. He imagines life on the run if he kills only her and not himself, wandering round winter seaside resorts until his money ran out . . .

He paces the bathroom seething, eyeing the key in the door that could release him; pacing back and forth across the blurry bath-mat until he can remember himself, his love for Ellen, his own name.

The outburst has come, as always, out of the blue – terrifying compared to his normal placidity. He returns at last from the bathroom with effortful apologies, which soon descend again into a kind of whine. Everything after this feels risky: he could crush her, break her, with just one more word. She has had enough. Yet everything he says to make up for it still comes out petulant.

Once the storm has passed, they chat more cheerily than *usual*! Ellen seems astonishingly cheerful, in fact no longer ill. But Owen has had a glimpse of the underworld: scratch the surface of his peaceful, polite demeanour and beneath all is molten guilt, despair, certainty of failure, indifference to life. Or is he just still angry?

You can hate a happy child, want to ruin its day that began so well, reject it, neglect it, break its favourite cup! Their fucking little fears, their endless needs! A child can drive you to the brim of the abyss. If we both died today, you think, it would save the world a lot of trouble. Death, the proof of your inability to love. Death your *reward*, parenthood your punishment.

You know those women who strap their children into car seats and let the car roll into a lake? You know those men who, in a fit of jealousy over a wife's infidelity, insist on killing the whole family as well as themselves: knives, poison, exhaust fumes, jumping off Beachy Head with a toddler under each arm? Well, Owen did none of that. He struggled on.

Ellen woke the next day and said she'd lost the will to live.

Does the cat think herself worthy, a being of infinite merit, and therefore entitled to the licking-into-shape? Or is she just uncomfortable in an untidy pelt? Is it the pleasure of licking, or a sense of personal honour, like a soldier in the trenches polishing his boots? Her *duty* to lick?

Owen wished he loved his life a little bit.

The smashing of babies' heads reflects the extent to which the dualism of anti-Semitic violence persisted, with secret, scientific killing proceeding alongside sudden, spontaneous acts of unspeakable cruelty . . .

He was a fine example of health, strength and youth. We were surprised by his cheerful manner. He looked around and said quite happily: 'Has anyone ever escaped from here?' It was enough. One of the guards overheard him and the boy was tortured to death. He was stripped naked and hung upside down from the gallows; he hung there for three hours. He was strong and still very much alive. They took him down and laid him on the ground and pushed sand down his throat with sticks until he died.

ELOÏSE

Birds that sing in the night are but few:
Nightingale,
Woodlark,
Less reed-sparrow,

Walking along in my bad-luck jumper, I think of myself as fleshless, skinless down one side, my body a cave of reddish, dripping ribs empty of organs.

I step on a basking bumblebee on a quiet path: the telltale crunch of its outer shell collapsing. Realizing I must have stepped on it, I go back to check and there is the struggling bee. Guilt-ridden, I leave the bee to its dying and turn a corner into a sunlit field where grasses twist, lingered by an invisible giant's hand: the world is beautiful. One bee short, but still beautiful.

Animals make the best of things. A horse is born a horse and makes do. No point in bemoaning the fact that it's not a bird. It's a horse! It's got a mane and tail and four legs. So it shakes that mane and makes a dash for it on the legs. A dash for what? Happiness.

To sit under a beech tree in spring, its young leaves still translucent. The branches shield me like a veil, trying to rest themselves on the ground. But when I leave, beech-nut husks crunch under my feet, forewarnings of death. *I will die before he comes to me.*

It was on a free trip to the States to see the Fall, courtesy of Hoover plc (what a swindle: the leaves hadn't turned yet, and the Hoover I had to buy to get the free tickets doesn't work properly), I found him. My poet. He was working in a bakery. At first I thought he meant he was a poet of *dough* – sonnets of baked goods lined the walls.

Customers came and went, merely mindful of their daily bread, while he filled my mouth with salted snakes and snails, sugared shells and stars. The soft forms he made for me. He gave me muffins made of mangoes and murmured in my ear – I seemed to stand in that bakery for days, watching the miracles and mysteries of manhood unfold.

Enough! he must have thought, we must introduce some harshness here. So he invited me to watch him play ice hockey. I had no idea what ice hockey *was.*

'The queen bee of team sports!' he claimed, astounded by my ignorance.

I hesitated, for I knew that as soon as I was alone in a dark car with this man I would want to put my hand on his thigh and my tongue in his mouth ... Knew too that he had a wife and probably a million other bakery-shop flirtations to nurture.

But I needn't have worried. In the car he was intent unswervingly on ice hockey: the game itself, numerous exciting manoeuvres he'd seen or carried out, the near slicing-off of his own ear under some blundering idiot's skate, the nature, purpose, glory and general *necessity* of this violent game. Talking fast, driving fast, hunched over his steering wheel, he made himself a stranger to me. I sat far away from him, hiding from his coldness.

The evening passed for me in an agony of hypothermia and anxiety on George's behalf. Glory indeed! A shuffle of great lumbering chaps awkwardly thrusting themselves about on ice (George's litheness, he later told me, was a great advantage against these huge padded opponents, who never knew where he was going to turn up next). Rushing and shoving like little boys round an unexploded World War II grenade. Bloody noses and unknown fractures, much scowling and set jaws: mock heroes for a mock battle. Given the chance, men create strife all round them. Bees would have had nothing to do with this, the bee's knees, be-all-and-end-all, of team sports! Bees do not gather together for purposeless displays of aggression.

Dizzy with cold and the ghastly game, I told George in the car park that I was relieved he had survived. He pulled me to him then and kissed me. With his mouth against my cheek, he said he loved my toes, my ankles, my legs, my wrists, my hair, my *nose* (it rhymed!). He sank to his knees, there between the cars, grabbed my hips, opened my coat, kissed my cunt through my dress, gathered me to him.

'Come,' he said later, at the hotel. 'I want you to come,' his hand like a boat navigating the undulations of my abdomen, making wave upon wave. 'Come.' I quickly reached a level of pain, of pleasure, he'd never envisaged (his power to make me weep from joy or sorrow).

In the days that followed he showed me sprays of red leaves on faraway hillsides throughout Vermont and New Hampshire, but what I remember is the way he turned me on the bed, pulled my face round to kiss him, his thumb in my mouth, his *voice*. With these offerings he condemned me to wander the earth forever after bewildered and unappeased: I could make no sense of a world in which I had to do without him.

How nonchalantly he abandoned me. Back to his wife, his life. It took me years to understand (for he never explained) that this was a matter of honour. Men are so ethical, they let us *die* for their principles! He knew a lot of things but not what to do with me. He wasted me, made my body a moral minefield, a no-man's-land. *I would have had his child, I would have had his child.*

How I loved him. But why? Because of his voice. Because of his poetry. Because he liked me but wouldn't act on it. Because he didn't always seem to like me. Because I don't like myself either. Because he didn't trust me but should have. Because I sensed beneath his coldness – and his kindness – that he loved me, which is why he stayed away.

How hateful the socks he sent to me (hockey socks!), along with a poem that was really a list of passionate promises. 'Come,' I replied by return of post, and for weeks I wore those socks as an emblem of our love: engagement socks! But as time passed and his repeated threats to arrive faded into more concrete plans to go elsewhere (he wrote wistfully of Montana and Istanbul), the socks became an emblem of my mistakes, my idiotic hopes, my oceanic despair, my unloved *feet*.

He will never touch me again.

He began to write as if we were old friends, but we were enemies. The antipathy I felt for all who knew him (even his customers), free-floating hatred and jealousy. He told me about a child he knew with an itchy bum. George found this hilarious. I didn't find it funny. I thought it quite possible the child had a serious medical disorder. I wanted him to talk of *our* children. Instead he sent a poem about a man walking across a street holding an imaginary child's hand.

How he played with me, lured me, tricked me. Why? Has he never felt the ground sink beneath him and continue sinking? He wrote me the most beautiful letters in the world and left me to lick the envelopes where he had licked, this jagged wound our only bond. (In the end, I plundered those envelopes for stamps to give the neighbour-boy: a small revenge.)

When my parents died, I stopped writing to him. It had become incomprehensible to me why people bother with each other at all. I felt *sorry* for anyone who loved. Love makes you vulnerable – vulnerable to *death*, that greatest unfairness of all. But none the less the loss of him merged with all the other deaths around me, a sea of people swiped from me.

O for him back again, O for him back again.

He has somehow got hold of my bag of worldly possessions. I am *dying* from this.

The landscape here seems to sag, flop, like me. It's not sturdy. In the sunken lanes, trees cling to a piece of earth or rock and squeeze it to death. I am touched by the slow growth of lichen (an inch per century). Six years is only a moment to lichen! George and I, in our different time zones, are as alike as a nub of grey lichen and the beating of a bee's wings: he has his fake strife, and I my hellish safety.

> On one occasion I saw two of these monsters (whales) prob-
> ably male and female, slowly swimming, one after the other,
> within less than a stone's throw of the shore ... over which
> the beech tree extended its branches.

GEORGE

An amazing light was shed on London tonight! I was in a taxi escaping from one of Venetia's dullsome dos, and from Kensington through Hyde Park to Westminster it followed us, this glorious GOLDEN LIGHT. The sun was hooded by a mauve-gray cloud that sent a piercing beam across the city, hitting trees and buildings horizontally. It was so beautiful, it almost made me cry, to think that human beings had erected this stuff – Parliament in particular, with its gold trim – just to catch this light, this once. The whole ballgame, the whole MESS humanity makes of everything, seemed, for fifteen minutes or so, JUSTIFIED. (And not so messy.)

I worry about Eloïse. There must be some way of finding her. Why'd she stop WRITING? Tired of my confusion? And the occasional long silence while I supposedly sorted myself out? She could be DEAD. Dying? Sick? Married to some aristocratic lughead? ANGRY? (Probably.) Sad??

But I had this crazy idea that if it was meant to happen it would happen, without my having to do anything much, or hurt anybody (my WIFE, for instance). Jesus, always trying to be GOOD, as if life were just one long trudge after moral RECTITUDE! Who do I think I am, George WASHINGTON? And for all my efforts to play the game by the rules, I still leave a trail of devastation in my wake. I'm a criminal at heart: Uncle Harry Hands' rightful successor.

She will wait forever, WON'T she?
Meet on the street one day and say, 'I LOVE YOU'?
All too LATE, too late now,
Near her but not WITH her, IN her.
Anguished by my own inaction.
Lost all sense of what I came for,
Who I am or what I'm born for.
What I mourn for: Eloïse.

Sometimes I want to hug someone so much I search the immediate vicinity for ANYBODY. Since I'm usually in my own BATHROOM, don't find anyone. I cross my arms in the air around an imaginary love object and the hug gets tighter and tighter until I want to crush my fists through my chest wall, grab a lung in each hand, and tear myself to shreds.

My absent student is my sole companion, her and her weird malaise.

CUTE MEN OF OUR TIMES

Joseph Faller Sr. stabbed his wife Florene 219 times because she stacked the refrigerator full of vegetables, *hiding the milk*, and he wasn't going to stand for that any more.

A man slashed his wife open with a carving knife and hung her heart out on the balcony to dry because she said he'd overcooked the pasta.

Britain's most boring man became boring when he was 14 years old and started collecting old copies of the *Radio Times*.

He now has them all. He also collects wind-up toys, every type of paper bag and the sticky labels off fruit.

A wasp, desperate for something wet and sweet, clings boldly to a mango moving swiftly through space. The fruit is one in a box of twenty being carried down Brick Lane on a man's shoulder: he is taking them home to his family.

But Brick Lane, the box, the shoulder, the family, all mean nothing to the wasp, who is acutely aware only of her separation from her own nest and has fastened herself for what seems to her an eternity to that drying drip of juice on the mango's side.

(from the absent student's notebook)

What is the point of labeling each individual piece of fruit? Buy the fruit, EAT the ad! We've carved a chunk out of the ozone, burned up all the rainforests, soon we won't be able to BREATHE, and all because we had to label each individual piece of fruit.

ELOÏSE

It filled but a minute. But was there ever
   A time of such quality, since or before ...

I look and see it there, shrinking, shrinking,
   I look back at it amid the rain
For the very last time; for my sand is sinking,
   And I shall traverse old love's domain
     Never again.

Each love affair has its one central memory. Incongruous items appear:
bicycles and ginger beer, my burp at tea with some boy's parents, sitting
on a pavement blotto from vodka, an off-putting surname and talk of
anal sex, a sore chin from too much kissing, the scald from babyhood
on a man's shoulder, an African stew made from tongue, sad and final
fumblings in a Spanish hotel, a walk on a beach with a dog. I was once
drawn in my bath by an artist with a curved prick ... Our biggest
romances boil down to this, flotsam and jetsam unworthy of recall.

For such trifles friends and family are forgotten, vows made, bills
paid, children begotten and a lifetime's discomfort endured in a bed
too small for two. For the sake of mere sexual attraction whole lives
are lived and lost – and afterwards you *hate* the bloke.

Quickly manufactured passions, between people who don't even like each other! I seem to be the first person in history who doesn't think about sex from one week to the next. Romans, Vikings and Visigoths thought about sex all day. Lenin, Hitler and Napoleon were probably thinking about sex all day. I can no longer understand the general fascination with it. And the further you get from it, the dimmer the details. Do women really care what a man's bum looks like? And if so, *why*? And why so much nakedness? Surely it's chilly and inhibiting (must be a throwback to prehistoric times). I can no longer remember how you get past the hurdle of someone else's intestinal gurgles, or the ugliness of genitals.

Yet for sex women put up with hairy ears and orders, the loo seat up, the nightly meal and mockery of women. For sex they put up with men who eat spaghetti straight out of the tin. For sex people risk their lives! Does no one fear AIDS? Am I the only person who fears *death*?

I want a child.

Scientists have abolished love. We're all in it for the sake of our genes. We weep for the smiles of children because we're *programmed* to. In anguish we languish, unwitting slaves to biology. But sexual love is but a pale imitation of the love between a mother and child (you don't choose your friends and family on the basis of what they *look* like!). A feeble thing concocted out of hormones, clothing, lies and a junk diet of pop songs, its shallowness confirmed every time someone says, 'There are plenty of fish in the sea': the assumption is that you can direct your desires at practically *anyone*! In an ideal world, love would mean more than that – even microscopic germs have *sex*.

All wasted on men anyway. *Can* they love? They are from a different *planet*, certainly a different timescale. Their only aim is to spread their seed far and wide. They are *born* to deceive, to deprive, to misunderstand, mislead, ignore and ruin women. Love is wasted, wasted on them.

Men are lonely, much lonelier than they realize. Their mistake is in spending too much time with other men: equals only in futility, they speak so that other men will hear and listen only to hear what other men say.

I hate them all! I hate them because they're married, I hate them for their aloofness, their hostility, their arrogance – the arrogance of people who don't *menstruate* (you can't be that proud of yourself if you run the risk of leaking bodily fluids in public every month). Men have no humility. This makes them dangerous. I want to kill, really *kill*, men who rape and murder. How could it be rational *not* to want to kill them?

And they dare to rule the world! They have made it so *ugly*. Square houses! Their obsession with straight lines and right angles has ruined the earth! They consider all curves, all subtleties, all softness, all indefinites, *female*, and they shun them. They have poisoned and denatured everything they touch, and expect us to be grateful.

I once found a butterfly sanctuary nearby. Never found it again. Either they redesignated it as farmland or what they'd designated was tinier than I thought. If it were up to me the whole *planet* would be a butterfly sanctuary, but leave it to men and butterflies get ten square feet.

Nuclear bombs, fluorescent lights, burning witches at the stake, deciding animals have no emotions – only men could have come up with such ideas. And they're so *messy:* oil spills follow them wherever they go! They've jammed the underwater sound waves with so much primitive sonar equipment and motor boats that whales can't navigate or even hear themselves *think*. Men will be our downfall. *They will take us all down with them.*

Love is wasted on them. They are miniaturists! So bogged down in trivia they never see the whole picture. The pettiness of my flat-mate, Howard, with his inventory of every teaspoon, right down to the old frayed clothes-peg bag! Complaining about the couch! The couch had survived two world wars, according to him, and then I'd wrecked it. How many more wars did he have *planned* for it? Him and his chintz.

People waste your time trying to convince you that men are reasonable, respectable, *human*. They're not. They're crap. Mutants. Bygones. Useless. Why won't anyone just *say* so? They shouldn't be let loose on the streets – they make life impossible for everyone, mugging and tormenting people ... They're crap. Slugs writhing in mud. Crap. Attention to detail. 'Sense of history'! Crap. Dullards, malingerers, gigolos, sycophants, boors – and that's the best of them! Poets. Parasites on women, betrayers all. None of them worth the socks they stick their big feet into. All crap. We should take them and their capitalist system and their so-called democracy and their ludicrous judges' wigs and their fucking Industrial Revolution and everything else they're so proud of and stuff it into one of their leaky nuclear-waste canisters and blow them all to *smithereens*, the great male death wish finally fulfilled. Crap. All.

They don't even believe women fart! They don't believe we piss whole pints of pee just like they do. They're ignoramuses, they invent the world to suit themselves, they don't really *want* to under-stand it. Slugs. They can only focus on tiny bits at a time. Train timetables, periodic tables, billiard tables! And all their lists! Even the best of their ideas are tainted by myopia. They invent things without a thought to the consequences, what heartache they may cause. Napalm, BSE, nuclear power stations leaking into the Irish Sea ... How can they *do* it? The man who released African killer bees in South America has apparently *forgiven* himself (hundreds of people have died). Their fog of self-satisfaction knows no bounds. Newsmen launch into *sports* news after news of air crashes, the slaughter of Hutus and Tutsis, the whereabouts of Nazi gold – with a smile. A *smile*.

And their hobbies! Trainspotting, birdwatching, stamp collecting, amateur photography (porn), remote-control airplanes, giant vegetables ... Why? *Why?* Only a man could think that getting a miniature plane off the ground was time well spent. And vegetables are better small. Not giant, *small*. The only possible reason for growing a giant vegetable is to prove (to anyone still in any doubt) that you are an utterly absurd and worthless human being with no recognizable function in this world.

Men seem suspiciously *eager* to prove this (my father's weird method of making beds saved him from ever being *asked* to make them). They seek to discourage any lingering notion that they might be people you can depend on. They *pride* themselves on their own futility, even award each other *prizes* for it: a prize here for growing a tuber too big to budge, a prize there for dragging yourself to the pub every night to throw darts. Purposeless pointless beings, *intent* on purposelessness. And forever *shooting* at things (with balls or bullets). They have all sunk into a realm of unreality because they cannot make babies and cannot make sense of a world in which they are so self-evidently *useless*. Crap. All of them. Crap. *Oh hold me honey push it into me take me take me fuck me now*. Useless. All utterly useless to *me*.

I like to think of past loves: one hanging by his prick, another by the fingers he failed to thrill me with, one poised for all eternity on his sharp bum bones, another sucked into the air by a toilet plunger attached to his flabby bald head. All vultures who came to pick at my carrion flesh once, now pierced, poised, impaled, dangling helplessly for ever as punishment for their ill-treatment of me.

No babies for me. No babies for me.

HOW EVERYTHING WRONG WITH THE WORLD IS MEN'S FAULT:

1 **Kleenex**. Man-size Kleenex is not only bigger but softer. They think women don't blow their noses. Men rule the world.
2 **Marilyn Monroe**. Men don't really believe that women *exist*. Marilyn Monroe died of this.
3 **Hobbies**. Activities characterized by futility, sanctifying madness.
4 **Whistling**. Men are forever announcing their presence with this territorial tunelessness. Their footsteps too are oppressive. They don't give women room to *breathe*.
5 **Cats**. Men have no understanding of cats. Cats are curvaceous and unwilling to be ordered about – men therefore have no patience with them.
6 **Male nipples**. Borrowed jewellery for a chest that is too flat. They even stuck nipples on their medieval armour! Ridiculous. *Insane*.
7 **Death**. Unable to make babies, they make bombs instead. Men menstruate by shedding *other* people's blood.
8 **Pollution**. If men didn't molest and abduct them, children could *walk* to school, thus saving on petrol.

9 **Men who catch butterflies**. Enough said. Ditto, men who steal eagles' eggs.

10 **Men who can't sew**. Or *won't*.

11 **Men who fight women as windmills**.

12 **Men of few words**.

13 **Bathroom tiles**. Men are always over-tiling things.

14 **Deprivation**. Men do not rest easy in their graves unless they have deprived every woman they have ever come into contact with of whatever she wanted from them.

15 **Purpose**. The only possible purpose in a man's existence is to make one woman happy. They all seem depressingly unaware of this.

16 **Lists**. Men have reduced the world to lists.

HOWARD

Howard's inventory of flat contents:

Howard's room: 2 floor mats

2 mahogany chairs

1 wooden towel rail

1 bedside table with cupboard

1 bookcase, small, wood

1 double bed with mattress and valance

1 table, kitchen type

2 bedside lamps with shades

1 x 13 amp extension lead

2 sets window curtains (swag)

1 x 2 kW electric heater

Eloïse's room: 1 floor mat

1 oak chair (fabric seat)

1 bookcase, white, painted

1 single bed, with mattress

1 set window curtains (bramble motif)

1 newspaper rack

1 small bookcase

1 bookcase attached to wall

	1 fire extinguisher
Hallway:	1 bookcase
	1 fire extinguisher
Sitting room:	1 floor mat
	1 hearth rug
	1 Chesterfield couch with bird-pattern, loose cover and 2 separate cushions
	1 wing easy chair with bird pattern, loose cover and 1 separate cushion
	1 mahogany chair
	1 oval gate-legged table
	1 bookcase (dark wood)
	1 table lamp with shade
	1 standard lamp with shade
	2 wall-bracket lamps with shades
	1 stereo radio with two speakers
	2 sets window curtains
	1 x 2 kW electric heater
	1 stuffed pike in glass case
	1 back-scratcher
In cupboard:	1 vacuum cleaner with tools
	1 ironing board
	1 iron
	1 clothes rack
	1 floor brush
	1 floor mop
	1 dustpan and brush
	5 glass preserve jars
Bathroom:	1 washing machine

1 x 13 amp extension lead for washing
machine

280 stacked tiles

1 set window curtains (abstract)

1 shower curtain and rail (fish pattern)

Kitchen: 1 rush mat

2 oak chairs (fabric seats)

1 armchair with cushion

1 dining table

1 refrigerator

1 refuse bin

1 fire extinguisher

1 fire blanket

2 sets window curtains (bramble motif)

1 doormat

1 small saucepan

1 medium   "   with lid

1 casserole with lid (stainless steel)

1 frying pan with lid

1 saucepan with lid, aluminium

1 preserving pan with lid, aluminium

1 ceramic casserole with glass lid

1 enamelled metal casserole

1 colander with lid

1 wire cake holder

1 toaster

2 large meat dishes

1 blender/coffee grinder

1 filter coffee pot and filter holder

1 hot-water jug (blue china)

1 teapot and mat

1 pepper mill

1 salt canister

1 tea caddy

1 coffee caddy

1 electric kettle

3 wooden chopping boards

9 wine glasses

5 tumblers

2 glass tankards (1 x ½ pt, 1 x 1 pt)

7 sherry-size glasses, assorted

3 milk jugs, various sizes

8 cereal bowls, small red

6 cereal bowls, large red

3 butter dishes, 1 glass, 1 metal, 1 china

1 sugar bowl with lid

6 egg cups, assorted

7 dinner plates, red

7 side plates, red

5 bread and butter plates

1 small glass bowl (e.g. for salt)

2 teacups and saucers, red

2   "   "   "   yellow

6 black coffee cups and 5 saucers

2 large glass bowls

2 china bowls, 1 blue, 1 yellow

1 Pyrex measuring jug

1 set scales, weights and separate pan

1 bag clothes-pegs and washing line

1 lemon-squeezer

2 wooden spoons

3 metal spoons

2 metal forks

2 tin-openers, 1 hand, 1 for wall

1 jar-opener

1 kitchen scissors

1 cheese-grater

1 egg-beater

1 potato-masher

1 soup ladle

1 tongs

1 knife-sharpener

1 tea-strainer

1 bottle-opener

1 rolling pin

1 corkscrew

1 nutcracker

1 carving fork

1 knife, steel

6 sharp knives

6 teaspoons

1 salt spoon

8 table knives

6 " forks

9 dessert spoons

2 tablespoons

1 flan dish

1 oval pie dish

1 sieve

1 mixing bowl, metal

1 mixing bowl, china

3 pudding basins

6 pastry-cutters

2 hot-water bottles

2 plastic bowls

1 wooden bowl

8 rush table mats

3 trays

1 concertina file containing inventory of flat
   contents

ED

We had in this village ... an idiot-boy ... who, from a child, showed a strong propensity to bees; they were his food, his amusement, his sole object ...This lad exerted all his few faculties on this one pursuit. In the winter he dosed away his time ... by the fireside, in a kind of torpid state ... but in summer he was all alert, and in quest of his game in the fields, and on sunny banks. Honey-bees, humble-bees, and wasps, were his prey wherever he found them: he had no apprehensions from their stings, but would seize them *nudis manibus*, and at once disarm them of their weapons, and suck their bodies for the sake of their honey-bags. Sometimes he would fill his bosom between his shirt and his skin with a number of these captives; and sometimes would confine them to bottles ...As he ran about he used to make a humming noise with his lips, resembling the buzzing of bees.

Ed sat on some lovely squishy cakes of mud and talked to his pumpkins. 'Someone's for it!' he warned them. The pumpkins hadn't been making sufficient progress. There had been no advance in their diameters since yesterday, none that he could detect anyway.

In his beloved shed Ed mixed a bowlful of his secret growth supplement, a combination of plant food, cow manure, Eco-

Phos-Pro-Bio tablets, cherry linctus and a number of his own bodily fluids. Ed delicately sprinkled this mixture beneath each pumpkin.

(His parents had named him Ed because it was only two letters and easy to spell.)

Then he set about the most dilatory pumpkin with a shovel, bashing through its rich shiny shell and beating it to a pulp as an example to the others. (Plant lessons must be kept simple.)

Ed had established himself by various means (not all of them wholesome or legal) as one of the leading names in the giant-vegetable-growing world. He had grown a 108-pound cabbage, a 53-pound beetroot, a lettuce that was 3 feet across and weighed 29 pounds. He had grown celery that was 5 feet high. With the help of his secret growth supplement and 43 bales of straw, 8 of peat and an extra pat or two of cow manure he had once managed to produce 493 potatoes from a single root! He had also been cultivating giant onions for many years, some the size of his own head.

Ed (who liked to shoot at the full moon with an illicit handgun each month, and made a living as a burglar in his spare time) went to have a quick look at his beehives. A woodpecker had been at them, drilling holes in the side and then just sitting there picking bees off when they rushed out to investigate. In his shed Ed unearthed an old plastic owl (his shed had everything) and nailed it to the fence beside the hives in the hope that a woodpecker would be wary of an owl, even an old plastic one. As he struggled to get it into a convincing, aggressive pose, bees settled tenderly on Ed's shoulders to bask in the sun.

He sang to them: 'I am the honey, honeysuckle, you are the bee. I like to take the honey from your sweet lips, you see.' He no longer ate them. He'd stopped doing that when he reached puberty.

None the less, he did sometimes chase them and liked to tease the queen. The bees were at his mercy.

> Leave the bumblebee in the killing-jar for at least half an hour
> ... If the oesophagus has been cut by first removing the bee's
> head, the whole honeystomach can be removed from the
> abdomen with a pair of forceps.

Ed went home and switched on his electric train set, then made a phone call, his telephone manner becoming more and more lewd as the train zoomed faster and faster through the tunnels. But the woman on the other end didn't seem unduly alarmed. (The stupidity of women astounded him. One neighbour once told him she'd seen a swarm of bees in his garden – *months* after she'd seen it! What use was that? What use was *she*?)

In bed that night, he recognized that he was lonely, much lonelier than he'd thought. Apart from his bees, pumpkins, root vegetables, train set, pipe bombs and the various clocks and musical instruments he'd stolen from people's houses, he was alone. No one knew of his many successes and failures, his birthdays, his plans for the future. He felt like a Japanese businessman holed up for the night in one of those ultra-modern hotels like beehives, with cells just big enough for the grubs (businessmen) to turn over: everything an inch from your head including sink, wardrobe, TV and breakfast. You know you're dead when everything's within arm's reach. But we're all single-cell organisms these days. Since the invention of the video and the telephone, people need never meet up again.

He went into the living room and wanked to a video on insect mating behaviour that included crowds of ladybirds fucking merrily

(*'Lesbians'*, chuckled Ed every time he watched it). Ed's genitals – gnarled knobs, wrinkly crinkly skin, veined, pimpled 'n' 'orrible, asymmetrically protruding from a bed of thick, tough hairs – reminded him of a carnivorous plant he'd once seen at Kew. In fact he'd *queued* to see it! Supposed to stink but didn't. What a con.

The Structure and Shape of the Fungus Fruit-body

Reproduction of Fungi

Classification of Fungi

The Life Cycle of Fungi

Distribution of Fungi

The Importance of Fungi for Man

On rainy days Ed kept himself to himself, busy manufacturing the letter bombs he sent to women in the News (Newswomen, women mentioned by Newswomen, women who happened to get in the way of a News camera, etc.). He had nothing against women per se, just women in the News. He'd never killed anyone yet. A few fingers had been blown off here and there. Pretty harmless really. He didn't *want* to kill them, just give them a fright. Like they'd given him.

He had spent seventeen years perfecting his letter bombs, or 'bomblets' as Kate Adie had once called them on the News after one little incident (or was it spelled 'bomelette' like 'omelette'? Ed ate a lot of those and often wondered about it).

Each bomb was constructed from hand-carved wooden elements and home-made screws so that they couldn't be traced to any shops. He even sanded off the serial numbers on the tiny batteries he used to ignite the fuse. They were beautiful little objects in their way, these bombs, but unfortunately so innocuous they never got the kind of publicity they deserved considering the craftsmanship involved in their creation.

The truth was, Ed wanted to stop his bombing campaign, his lonely mission to save the world from women in the News. It had ceased to satisfy him. He was tired of travelling to distant deserted postboxes, wearing sunglasses, not even able to get a cup of *tea* in case someone remembered and could identify him. He had evaded detection with such ease that he had grown tired of anonymity, tired of success! – and longed to be released from his self-imposed solitude in which newspapers were his primary companions, newspapers full of women. (Doing without the News was not an option. He *panted* in anticipation of the next disaster. And he was not alone in this. There is global excitement about death in double figures.)

Some of Ed's many successes:

Beetroot : 53 lb 8 oz
Broccoli : 25 lb
Cabbage : 108 lb
Calabrese : 16 lb
Carrot : 15 lb 7 oz
Celery : 26 lb 1 oz
Corn cob : 26¼ in
Courgette : 44 lb 8 oz
Cucumber : 10 lb 1 oz
Garlic : 2 lb 10 oz
Green bean : 48 in
Leek : 12 lb 2 oz

Marrow : 78 lb 2 oz
Onion : 12 lb 4 oz
Parsnip : 71¼ in
Potato : 7 lb 13 oz
Pumpkin : 406½ lb
Radish : 32 lb 7 oz
Squash : 375 lb 5 oz
Swede : 42 lb 3 oz
Tomato : 7 lb 12 oz

CONCLUSION TO PART ONE

MANGO vs. MAN

In what way is a man more than a mango?

Is he more useful about the house?

Is he more beautiful?

Is he as generous and obliging as this succulent fruit gently ripen-
ing on your window sill?

Is his ripeness as tender?

Will your children like him as much as they'd like a mango?

Has he got anything to offer in atonement for *not* being a mango?

Mangoes do not lord it over everybody at committee meetings.

Nor do they monopolize the conversation at dinner.

With even the most lethargic of men, there is still the threat of
physical force.

Not so with a mango.

A mango's ears do not stick out.

A woman does not have to wear lipstick and high heels in order
to spend an evening with a mango.

A woman does not have to wash her hair for a mango.

I have only known one mango that was no good.

(from the absent student's notebook)

Part Two
Connemara

All memory of the old home, its needs, conditions, and duties is cancelled, and the new communal identity proceeds to embark on the adventure of life without delay. Even the situation of their late home is effaced from memory.

An inquest was held on the 8th inst., on the body of Mary Cunningham, of Carrickbanagher . . . Verdict—"died for want of sufficient food."

An inquest was held, same day, upon the body of James M' Garry, at Ardcurly. Verdict—"died of insufficiency of food and clothing to support life."

An inquest was held on the 9th instant on the body of Patrick Ward, Tunagh. Verdict—"deceased came to his death by starvation."

An inquest was held on the 13th inst., on the body of Michael Kilmartin, Emero. Verdict—"deceased came to his death by starvation."

An inquest was held same day, on the body of Catherine Kilmartin, of Emero. Verdict—"died of want of food."

An inquest was held same day, on the body of Bridget M'Dermott, of Doonskeen. Verdict—"died of want of food."

An inquest was held same day, upon the body of Patrick Dyer, Ardagh. Verdict—"died of starvation and want of proper clothing."

An inquest was held at Aughanah upon the bodies of Edward Tighe, John Tighe, and Anne Tighe—brothers and sister. Verdict—"died of starvation and want of proper clothing."

The Vindicator, Belfast, 20 January 1847

ELOÏSE

My favourite cat has died and my house has been burgled. A speeding car ran over the cat and broke her back, just outside on the lane. She was still breathing, so I took her to the vet, yelling at her all the way to live.

Returned, minus cat, to find a police car outside my house. The neighbours had called them when they noticed a window had been broken. But not only had I been burgled, I'd been incompletely burgled. My parents' papers were strewn everywhere – a sea of papers – and my clock and my cello were gone. Eventually, the police *found* the clock beside the broken window: the burglar must have been disturbed as he was leaving (perhaps by the neighbours), panicked, and left the clock behind. But he took the clock *key*, so now I can't wind it. But why do I need to know what time it is? I know all too well it's too late, *too late*.

The neighbours are thrilled – their every new D.I.Y. window lock has been vindicated. While I lie here in a pool of parents' papers, papers designed to overwhelm the soul.

Why couldn't the world just leave me alone, me and my little clock and my little cat?

> In the roads lie the broken spears . . .
> Without roofs are the houses,
> And red are their walls with blood.

Maggots swarm in the streets and squares,
And the ramparts are spattered with brains.
The waters have turned crimson, as if they were dyed,
And when we drink them they are salty with blood.

'Anyone wishing to pick her nose should do so now,' said Eloïse's father as the car entered another tunnel on their trip through Switzerland.

Childhood is a swindle, a very unequal bargain. There was Eloïse, poor mummy-infatuated kid, in ecstasies of devotion at her mother's side, loving her mother's face, the most important face in the world, her voice the most important voice, her hands the only hands, the way she did things the only way, her *things* the best *things*: her perfume, her shoes, her handbag, her black coffee, her cigarettes, her watch, her aprons, her lipstick, her songs, her stodgy puddings and slavish adherence to the notion that there must be meat and two veg every night . . .

And there was Eloïse's mother, exasperated beyond bearing with this clingy child and twelve years spent opening tins when she could have been writing poetry. The daily vigil of keeping a child alive and happy, a child that was often to be found masturbating behind the sitting-room settee, a child that persisted in secretly festooning her bedroom wall (in one particular spot near her pillow) with nose-pickings, a child that was always a little too plump, shy, weepy, and behind with her schoolwork.

Eloïse sensed (not without some bewilderment and anger) that she was not allowed to love her mother as much as she wanted. She was too demanding a child. When her mother became ill, Eloïse took it as a punishment for her too-great love. She must learn not to burden her mother with love. She must learn never to depend on her mother, and never again to take love to extremes. Her love could *kill*.

She clung to what was left of her mother (who sometimes miraculously surfaced from illness like a mermaid for air). But Eloïse always felt she lacked vital divulgences, even vocabulary, which mothers pass on to their daughters. She hardly knew what these gaps in her education were, but one was: Do you love me? Another: What does one do with soda crystals?? And because her mother never told her these things, ignorance and deprivation would be handed down the generations: Eloïse would not be able to love her own children or tell them things.

To preserve what was left of infancy, Eloïse went on reading children's books well into her twenties, returned home after university to tend her parents, and never quite took to coffee. (Babar the Elephant's orphan childhood particularly moved her.)

Her father made up the housework as he went along. It was a rather haphazard business. The only thing he liked to cook was ice cream, and even that usually had little undissolved lumps of gelatin in it that were hard to swallow. He was a willing hooverer though, and enjoyed shopping: bottle-brushes were his greatest find.

But if the truth be told, most housework can be omitted without grave consequences.

Most popular songs at funerals:
1 'I Will Always Love You'
2 'My Way'
3 'In the Mood'
4 'Smoke Gets in Your Eyes'
5 'Imagine'

Grandma hates women (herself included). She seems to think they count for nothing. She was only ever interested in her paunchy husband, her paunchy husband's business, her paunchy husband's paunchy frame and the unfairness of his early death. For years she made my father wear his father's old suits (taken in by the tailor but still humiliatingly out-of-date), and doused him daily in her scorn.

When my parents eloped to London to evade her wrath, Grandma jumped to the conclusion that my mother, being Catholic, must be pregnant. They eventually made a dutiful wedding visit back to Connemara, where my father lapsed into the torpid state he maintained whenever he was with his mother, and failed to notice for quite a while that she had reduced his bride to tears with all her talk of feckless Catholic cleaning ladies.

My parents took up permanent residence in London, intending never to return. But when I was born a few years later, a telegram appeared at the hospital, saying 'I FORGIVE YOU'. My mother had just had an emergency Caesarean and had no interest in being forgiven. But thus began a steady strained acquaintance, from which I at first benefited – Grandma gave good presents. She once gave me a doll that talked! My mother hated that doll.

Every few years we would trek out to see Grandma, staying at the near by Rossadilly Hotel for a week or two. Rossadilly: donkeys in the field smelling of tarragon, puppies in the barn, boats on the lake, green grass meeting blue water all round me, porridge for breakfast, strange orange juice from a tin, and Grandma a barely remembered afternoon chore.

To my surprise the Chanukkah presents stopped coming when I reached thirteen (I was supposedly an adult). Grandma's affection for me just as abruptly dried up. Then my mother went into hospital again and my father had to spend all day watching amateurish doctors muck her about (one neurosurgeon managed to paralyse her permanently down one side). I was shipped off to stay with Grandma until things improved. She criticized my hair, the way I dressed, the way I ate (too much cheese), my bralessness, my poor posture, my ignorance of make-up, my interest in Guinness, my exam results, my day-long wanderings (which she dubbed my 'escapades'), my silence, my shyness and my vague desire to see Galway. But most of all, she criticized my mother − for being ill. Her main concern was the effect of my mother's illness on my *father*: whether or not my mother would ever be able to relieve him of his household duties.

I slept on the couch and wept in the bathroom. For months I listened to that woman's whining and the hourly attempts of her three chiming clocks to make contact in that loveless house. There was no colour anywhere, only dampness and every shade of grey.

My mother finally came out of hospital and I returned home. She was barely recognizable but she was my mother still. One night, I found the nurse yanking her off the commode by her *breasts*, making my mother cry.

I never forgave Grandma for any of it.

> Little or nothing is doing to relieve the sufferers. By this time fever has made its way into almost every house. The poor creatures are wasting away and dying of want. In very many instances the dead bodies are thrown in waste cabins and dykes and are devoured by dogs. In some parts the fields are bleached with the bones of the dead . . .

The postman wakes me from a dream in which I'm walking down a grassy gravelly lane, walking into the *past*: Memory Lane. I can walk down it or turn at any time and go back to the *present*, where I've left the car.

I have slept the whole night on the unassuageable bones of my parents, lying on the floor still covered with their lifetimes' papers. It isn't easy getting *up*. I go to the door (once the postman has gone) and there on the mat is a letter from Grandma's solicitor belatedly informing me of her death (he had difficulty tracking me down). I have been awarded yet more ill-gotten gains: her hideous hunting lodge in beautiful Connemara, wretched remnant of her tirades and tyrannies.

Now I realize what was so familiar about that lane in my dream, lined on each side by long grass with a wide white sky beyond. It was the lane to the Rossadilly Hotel.

Derravonniff – piglet wood

Lettermuckoo – the hillside of pigs

Derreennagusfoor – the small wood of the cold feet

Sheeauns – the fairy hills

Griggins – the lumpy or pebbly places

Mace – buttock (a broad, elevated area)

Snauvbo – swimming-place of cows

Keeraunnagark – the moorland hill of the hens

Gooreenatinny – the fox's small sandbank

Coorhoor – the uneven road

Lemnaheltia – the leap of the doe

Shannanagower – the slope of the goats

Gorteennaglogh – small field of stones

ELOÏSE'S GRANDMOTHER

... the aged queen often spends the evening of her life very pleasantly with her little band of worn-out workers. They sit together on two or three cells on top of the ruined edifice ...

Widowhood was hard to bear. It had now taken the form of constipation. A laxative treatment involving senna pods had had a violent effect – all over her clothes and the bathroom floor. The epitome of solitude, cleaning up one's own shit (no one evades this responsibility). She was mopping it up off the floor when she heard a loud trumpet sound behind her. Whizzing round in surprise, she found that it was her own bottom that had trumpeted and, in turning, she had splattered another whole wall.

Soon after this, she slipped on a wet stone on her way to the neighbours' farm to get mutton for Susie-cat. The incident wasn't frightening, only irritating. She fell so slowly she had ample time to anticipate the inevitable injury, but not to prevent it, and in her attempt to buttress herself with her right arm she split a bone in her wrist.

The indignities of such an injury, the difficulties faced by an old woman trying to bathe, pee, dress herself, open tins and manage the kettle, one-handed; the worry of having to keep the plaster cast dry for six weeks in that damp house, in that soft rain (or else get to hospital for a new one); the infuriating questions people asked about whether she was right- or left-handed – what did *they* care? She did manage to bathe, but getting dressed took hours.

She was chopping wood one day, holding the axe with difficulty under her *arm*, when the Calor-gas man suddenly appeared behind her. Hard to know who was the more alarmed, the great burly chap or the mad axe-lady!

Trips twice a week to hospital by minibus once the cast was off, for 'physiotherapy'. What good was it? But 'One must just be as cheerful as possible about these things', as she told her fellow beleaguered passengers.

'Would you try to make a fist for me, please?' asked the handsome young doctor.

'Oh, I'd do anything for *you*, Doctor,' she replied, but immediately regretted flirting with him, for he seemed embarrassed (and she couldn't make a fist anyway).

She no longer recovered from things. Nothing healed. Instead she had learnt to reshape her life around each new, permanent sign of deterioration. A heating pad. Handlebars in the loo. A rubber bath mat, its suckers pressed determinedly into her tub by a social worker. Loose clothing that could be pulled by a weak right wrist over an aching left shoulder ... But the bath mat was the worst. Horrid pink thing! A bath was not the same with that thing in there. She had hoped never to sink to this – but the combination of soap and soft peat water had become lethal.

Long-widowed, estranged from her son and son's family, holed up in a remote corner of a country that had never cared for her. Her only companion: Susie-cat, who at twenty and a half had begun to pee on carpets at night. It was a race to see which of them would die first.

Sometimes, out shopping, the old lady would waylay strangers to gripe to. She complained to them of blacks, Arabs and other sad things. But she tired of these newfound companions quickly. She was really only interested now in other widows.

That she should have sailed so far and for so long on the port tack with her jib and foretopmast staysail set on the starboard tack is not as improbable as it may sound.

OWEN

Owen hated taking unnecessary risks with Ellen's life, so abruptly entrusted to his care. He was reluctant to buy a car at all: they're so prone to accidents, life and death hanging on a moment's loss of concentration or a flat tyre. He didn't use his car unless he absolutely had to, preferred Ellen not to be in it, hated even more for her to be in someone else's – no one could possibly drive as carefully as he did.

He worried about her diet, which consisted these days mainly of monosodium glutamate: crisps and instant Chinese noodle soup. He worried about her sleep pattern, or lack of one. She wouldn't go to bed early enough, then had trouble getting up in time for school. She also woke in the night and dreamed things that bothered him. Lately she had been sleeping in his bed, after seeing a programme on telly about alien abductions. She wasn't going to let that happen to *her* out of earshot! (Though what could Owen have done about an alien abduction?) She would lie there reading for hours, too frightened to fall asleep until he joined her.

He worried about her at school all day with teachers he barely knew. What if they were cruel to her? What if she vomited (as he had) and became the laughing-stock of the class for ever? Anything could happen when she was out of his control, anything.

Owen now thought he knew why some mothers stay at home all day. It's not to catch up with the housework and soap operas – it's just so that they can worry about their offspring non-stop, without the interruptions of some silly job. He too would have liked to stay at home all day worrying, in fact on some level he half-believed that if he *stopped* worrying, Ellen might not *survive*. But he had a job to go to – as a council committee clerk, taking the minutes of adoption-panel meetings. All day he was distracted from worrying about his own child by having to listen to bureaucrats discussing other children's fates; each case was treated as if the child (why not the adoptive parents?) was doomed from the start, its life already a hopeless enterprise, badly conceived and executed. Orphans and abuse victims were left to languish in unsafe institutions while tetchy windbags squabbled over the ethics of non-ethnic placements, single parenthood, poverty, lesbian love nests – and, worst of all, whether or not the children had 'anything in common' with their adoptive families. Absurd, when the bond between a parent and a child is such a jumble of *imponderables* – a committee of eight or eighty could never figure it out! Owen (who knew more about single parenthood than anyone else in the room) was never allowed to speak. It was truly a form of torture. His life only began at home – once Ellen was safely there.

He had always been wary of air travel, but the fear had become acute since Ellen was born. He would rather have her die in a car crash on land than permit the remotest chance of her falling alone through the sky.

He hated the present plan too. He was scared of the sea, mother of all mistakes. Its impenetrable ruminations. To take Ellen (who herself was scared of sharks) on a ferry, put her to sleep deep in its bowels . . . Just the thought of all that black fumbling water – you lose your bearings, lose touch with gravity, gliding insensibly through the sludge of a night-time sea.

He watched the lorries being loaded ahead of him. The terrible size of the things and, presumably, the weight. Each must be an added liability, dragging the ferry down. '*Ro-ro-ro*' your boat: Roll on, Roll off, Roll over. That was what was said after the Zeebrugge ferry sank in three minutes.

The car park was almost empty except for a few lads playing a dilatory game of football and a poor half-blind dog who seemed to keep getting in their way looking for a safe place to sit. As he watched the sad old dog from his sealed car, with Ellen asleep in the back seat, all Owen could hear was his own swallowing. Not for the first time, he wondered if other people swallow as deafeningly.

He tried to remember if he had ever not been frightened of water. He'd been forced to learn to swim at school, despite his certainty that he was too thin to float. Caves, grottoes, bottomless lakes, unlit water creeping through crevices unknown . . . No, these things were and had always been terrifying. Nothing to do with his wife.

He found the bravery of lifeboat crews deeply moving. The thought of them setting off in sorry weather out of empathy for other people's distress, joining people in their watery tragedies just so that they wouldn't have to drown alone, adding terror to terror, atrocity to atrocity, all out of a sense of duty – never failed to bring a tear to his eye (though he had a lingering suspicion that they would not sacrifice everything, might not even get out of bed, to save *him*).

In the free element beneath me swam,
Floundered and dived, in play, in chase, in battle,
Fishes of every color, form, and kind;
Which language cannot paint, and mariner
Had never seen; from dread Leviathan
To insect millions peopling every wave ...

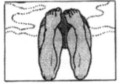 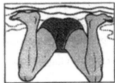 

THE EVIL DOCTOR

There is about 4000 persons in this parish, and all Catholics, and
as poor as I shall describe, having among them no more than --

> One cart,
>
> No wheel car,
>
> No coach, or any other vehicle.
>
> One plough,
>
> Sixteen harrows,
>
> Eight saddles,
>
> Two pillions,
>
> Eleven bridles,
>
> Twenty shovels,
>
> Thirty-two rakes,
>
> Seven table-forks,
>
> Ninety-three chairs,
>
> Two hundred and forty-three stools,
>
> Ten iron grapes,
>
> No swine, hogs, or pigs,
>
> Twenty-seven geese,
>
> Three turkeys,

Two feather beds,

Eight chaff beds,

Two stables,

Six cow houses,

One national school,

No other school,

One priest,

No other resident gentleman,

No bonnet,

No clock,

Three watches,

Eight brass candlesticks,

No looking-glasses above 3d. in price,

No boots, no spurs,

No fruit trees,

No turnips,

No carrots,

No clover,

Or any other garden vegetables, but potatoes and cabbage, and
not more than ten square feet of glass in windows in the whole,
with the exception of the chapel, the school house, the priest's
house, Mr Dombrain's house, and the constabulary barrack.

Facts from Gweedore: with Useful Hints to Donegal Tourists,
Dublin, 1845

He was of Anglo-Irish British-colonialist stock, with leanings to be different. His mediocrity (a dangerous trait in a doctor) didn't trouble him; his main cause for concern was his wife's face. He stared peevishly at it across the sticky table in the ferry's stinking cafeteria.

She'd had an angelic quality when they first met. He'd seen the light! – in her sparkling black hair, and her eyes when she looked up at him. It had satisfied any remnant he had of a religious urge. He'd seen in her a spiritual realm, she had a *radiance* (he hadn't realized it was simply because she was in love and still young).

Sometimes he thought he could see the same radiance in his children, though the boys never spoke and the girl was prematurely agog about sex. Watching the three of them now, chomping through their fish fingers, he thought he detected an afterglow.

He told himself repeatedly, especially when copulating with her, that his wife had once been beautiful. He also reminded himself that she was Egyptian, which made her an exotic specimen of some sort. But it was small comfort. He had begun to think of her as 'ugly', and he couldn't get the word out of his head. It was *embarrassing* to have an ugly wife – he saw the way people winced at the mismatch, such a negligible woman with such a handsome man. He was an Adonis, he couldn't help it (plenty of women had told him so in the privacy of the surgery or, preferably, in their own homes). In the meritocracy of physical attributes his wife was beneath him. She was aware of it herself. Wan, worn, her hair now more white than black (while yellow curls were still abundant on his head), and various blemishes becoming ever more pronounced. He would never knowingly have married someone with such bumps!

To compensate she made herself indispensable about the house:

she took the kids to their respective schools every morning, went home and made the beds or whatever women do, ran errands for him the rest of the day, typed things up for him at night. She also made a little money from teaching Arabic, and now, astonishingly, was pregnant again.

The ferry lurched unpleasantly. *Why did I marry?* A heavy month lay ahead for him, the annual challenge of avoiding his family. His theory was that Ireland accommodated all their needs: his, to stand on a golf green or in the bar discoursing on his Irish heritage; and hers, to supervise the children in seaside activities, as his mother had and other mothers before that. Never mind that the beach was covered at this time of year with dead jellyfish and it rained every day. It was *soft* rain, as he kept telling her.

THE 3 OLD BIDDIES

Logistics of manoeuvring 3 old biddies on to a bus. Suitcase in the way. Child cycling past. One biddy down. Another inserts herself bravely between prostrate biddy and bus, anchoring her feet against the kerb. Any minute now, they'll each break a hip and spend the whole holiday getting new ones.

But in the end they board the bus, old loves in their new shoes.

Endless conversation topics: food, health, grandchildren, sex, death, TV, politics, weather. Any remaining gap to be filled with gynaecology.

Off to Ireland, dimpled and giggling. And always somewhat bored. Stoical. Existences lacking in purpose. But, with any luck, the trip will pass in a blur of false mirth, three naughty girls on a spree.

ED

Ed couldn't believe his luck, chosen at the last minute to represent his county at the Connemara Vegetable Show! He had endured a few suspenseful days until it became clear that his only rival was already booked to go to the International Pumpkin Association's World Championship Finals in Santiago the same week. The local branch of the Giant Vegetable Growers' Confederation of Great Britain therefore decided that Ed could go to Connemara.

The hotel room would be free. All he had to do was lock up his valuables (he'd recently acquired someone's cello), heave the old pumpkin into the back of the van, and proceed to Ireland. (He'd once worked as a long-distance lorry driver so was well able to cope with any foreigners and foreign nonsense that crossed his path. That didn't worry him at all.)

His excitement was intense. He could barely contain himself, and anyway didn't have to: he stopped every hour to pee on his pumpkin (an old pumpkin-preservation trick), and to make certain that it was still regally positioned amongst its cushions. He had every confidence in its surviving the journey (his pumpkins usually lasted months) and in its doing well at the show. He was looking forward to beating the Paddies on the giant pumpkin front. He'd surely win a trophy and maybe even a bottle of Paddy's Irish whiskey! As he drove he pampered and peed upon his pumpkin, and practised his Irish jokes: 'How many Paddies does it take to change a lightbulb?' 'Lightbulb!? Since when did they have electricity?'

But the pumpkin didn't laugh. The pumpkin had only one thing on its mind: to spread its seed far and wide.

Welcome to the

Rossadilly Hotel

OFFERING:

Dinner, bed and breakfast

Bar, restaurant, room service

Nightly entertainment

Guided perambulations

Golf, tennis, swimming, riding, boating, angling,

scuba-diving, trips to the islands, croquet

Wine tasting

Friday-night quiz

Murder-mystery weekends

Lectures

Slide presentations

Bridge

Annual Connemara Vegetable Show

Group discounts

GEORGE

...Thus the whole circle of travellers may be
reduced to the following *heads*:

> Idle Travellers,
>
> Inquisitive Travellers,
>
> Lying Travellers,
>
> Proud Travellers,
>
> Vain Travellers,
>
> Splenetic Travellers,

Then follow

> The Travellers of Necessity,
>
> The delinquent and felonious Traveller,
>
> The unfortunate and innocent Traveller,
>
> The simple Traveller,

And last of all (if you please) The Sentimental
Traveller (meaning thereby myself) ...

Never mind clip-on curtains, Agas, sun-dried tomatoes, cranberries,
Prozac, old chipped enamel colanders, butlers' sinks, kelims,
anything Tuscan or terracotta (or preferably both), Dalmatians,
HRT, square pillows, mobile phones, bouquets of spaghetti or
gnarled twigs ... The latest English middle-class fad is IRELAND.

Venetia told me. She wants to send me there! Turns out she doesn't need to FUCK me after all (hooray), just wants to be my PATRONESS, *à la* Lady Gregory. She's heard about some dopey Murder Weekend at an Irish hotel, thinks it might inspire me. To what, I ask. *MURDER?*

Good ol' Venetia. Seems my supreme patience with her – first as appalled but outwardly supportive teacher, then as self-hating LAPDOG – has paid off! Of course I've accepted the offer, but I ain't going all that way for a weekend. My hope is to retreat TOTALLY from the WORLD, surround myself with the bleached bones of the few Irish poets who didn't manage to die in exile, and finish my poem. Find PEACE IN A CULTURED LAND (maybe even look up some Hanafans). In other words: take old V.'s money and run.

Nothin' to keep me HERE after all. Finally had news about my best student: not AWOL. Dead. Got hit by a car the very night I yelled at her in the street. Right *afterwards*, for all I know! *All my fault.* I have to LIVE with this. The car threw her into the air. 'Never felt a thing,' they say.

I think she felt a lot of things (some of them for *me*). I think we were probably made for each other! And now it's too late. Too late.

She's left me her notebook, my guilt and my imaginings.

ELOÏSE

The cloud of bees drifts and wheels in a seemingly aimless manner, and then it is seen to concentrate at a definite point, commonly on the branch of a tree. A few bees settle, others join them, and then we see the flying life flow together into one bunch of clinging bees the size of a pear, no, a cokernut . . .

Why do people travel? To see themselves in a new light, or an old one? Or is it just another form of *unconnectedness?* Hermits can travel. I must see Connemara again before I follow my father into his D.I.Y. death.

But am I to die *now?* The plane is shifting in the sky as if it too can't believe that planes work. I do not want to be here! I don't want to be on this plane (the curious phenomenon of vertigo, a mile high).

When we're finally disgorged, I feel like I've been inside a great fish's belly for three days. Trembling, I join the immobile crowd transfixed by the luggage carousel. People stare at the bags as if by force of will they'll turn into the right ones. You begin to get to know these bags after a few revolutions, take a tender interest in how they'll twirl round the corners.

Someone's forever trying to swindle you when you're travelling. Hiring a car always sounds easier than it is: as soon as I get to the firm's booth in the airport, they bombard me with questions until I'm too confused to realize I'm paying a second time for petrol I'd already bought by credit card in England ... But the long empty drive to Connemara calms me.

> The queen may be one of the first to join the cluster,
> but she is equally likely to be one of the last.

I never noticed in childhood that the roads of Connemara are bordered by fuchsia hedges growing wild. Creamy-coloured cows lounge proudly on the cliff tops, and all round me green grass meets blue water. When the scarlet bushes part, a white and grey hotel appears.

By the time I reach the hotel, I'm in an ecstasy of remembering. The white signpost that directs you to the tennis courts and swimming pool. The lake ... One cloudy day my father took us out on the lake in a rowboat and one of us fell in. It must have been *me* – I remember being wet. Now two colourful boats bob at the little jetty and the lake is a blur of wind-ruffled water.

The old forgotten smell of turf fires draws me into the hotel. Wood panelling and plaid settees. The view from my room is the same as it always was. Perhaps it's the same room? I slump into an armchair like an old lady unused to pleasure. Through the window that shudders slightly in the sea breeze come the smells of Rossadilly.

Everything is so vivid to a child. They're receptive because they're ignorant: they have no idea what a great swindle is in store for them. This is why their smiles move us so. (But it's the smiles of *adults* that should move us. *How can they smile?*)

It is a terrible thing to return to childhood as what I now am, shy, desperate, my life commandeered by hopeless adult struggles: lipstick worries, avoiding eye contact in the dining room, dreading the necessary encounters with the receptionist, and nursing a wrenched old-lady shoulder (the result of heaving too many bags round airports).

I tramp to the stables behind the hotel, hoping to find the same dog and her puppies that were there when I was six. *Never go back.* Even the donkeys are gone from the field behind, replaced by horses and properly scheduled riding lessons. In the old days, you could ride a donkey if you could catch it (not so easy).

I set off for Clifden for Nurofen for my neck. On the way, a sign for 'HAND KNITS' catches my eye. I turn my head with difficulty to look at the house. There are two cars for sale in the front garden and a jumper crucified in every window: someone's whole life has been turned into a souvenir shop.

The same could be said of Clifden (all flannel nightshirts, postcards and mittens) but it does have Nurofen – on special offer! I take two immediately and head back along the agonizingly bumpy road to Rossadilly.

Inside the hotel there are children everywhere. A plump couple having coffee and scones on a soft-hued couch. Turf fires and quiet talk. Could I be happy here? Briefly *happy*?

After collecting my key, still in pain, I walk stiffly to the stairs where I turn and find – how convenient – the doctor who killed my parents. Beside him, a pregnant woman. Is it wise to breed from murderers? His ugly smile vanishes when he recognizes me – he knows he's a killer. But he need not fear me. My mother taught me to be abjectly polite, but I was *born* a coward. I nod and skirt round them.

...a List of the Summer Birds of Passage which I have discovered in this neighbourhood, ranged somewhat in the order in which they appear.

Wry-neck,

Smallest willow-wren,

Swallow,

Martin,

Sand-martin,

Black-cap,

Nightingale,

Cuckoo,

Middle willow-wren,

White-throat,

Red-start,

Stone curlew,

Turtle-dove,

Grasshopper-lark,

Swift,

Less reed-sparrow,

Land-rail,

Largest willow-wren,

Goat-sucker, or fern-owl,

Fly-catcher,

GEORGE

I have heard the pigeons of the Seven Woods
Make their faint thunder, and the garden bees
Hum in the lime-tree flowers; and put away
The unavailing outcries and the old bitterness
That empty the heart.

Following, intermittently reverent, in the Great Man's footsteps, I wander the maze of paths at Coole. Duly inspect the tree trunk where every Irish literary bigwig seems to have carved his or her initials (Shaw's are the most lavish and savage, great scars gouged in the poor tree to satisfy his ego).

Something dutiful, not wholly VOLUNTARY, in my walking. Partly because I was ORDERED to see all *seven* woods by the young woman in the Information Centre, whose make-up seemed to be half-on, half-off: I was scared it might come *with* me (Exit, followed by face powder). Maybe she thought I was a more ardent Yeats fan than I am. I actually HATE visiting such shrines, don't know what I'm DOING here. But at least it's not as bad as Gilbert White's house in Selborne, where a life-size model of GILBERT stands frozen in the middle of his bedroom, just about to write a letter to some pal about a bird.

Site of Coole House

The Hothouse Garden

Back Lawn

Coole River

Bats

Turlough and Horse Pump

Ha-Ha

The Deer Pen

The Stone Seat

Dry Stone Walls

The Stable Yard

The Lime Kiln

Lichens

So fucking picturesque (that Yeats was no fool) I'm sort of relieved to find something *ugly*: a low drab building in a clearing. Boy is it ugly. No doors or windows that I can see. Appearing so suddenly among the trees, it looks like a mini-Buchenwald! (Why do I associate all forests with CONCENTRATION CAMPS? Fucking Germans.) Turns out to be the toilets. Men in one side, women in the other. ('Women to the right, men to the left!' the soldiers yell in *Schindler's List*). People are DEHUMANIZED by an overconcentration on gender (dehumanized by Hollywood movies too).

I sit on a toilet seat encrusted with ancient shit and think of all the shit the Jews had to die in, the shit IRA prisoners smeared across their walls, the shit strewn through history like the pink the British spread across the map of the world (the pink they should have blushed to spread). All the cruelty, the pain, the sorrow. Where does it END UP, this shit? Does it ever go? Does it just wash away?

I guess it does. IN THE END. I wipe *my* end, try the flusher – doesn't work – and leave.

With weird ease I drive on to Yeats's mythic TOWER just a few miles down the road. Pretty darn cute. I climb up the spiral staircase to his bedroom and stare at the bed he and his wife shared: I am constantly ENCROACHED on by COUPLES and their COUPLINGS. Empty, the heart.

Deafened by a blast of pre-recorded Yeats info that comes out of the walls whenever an unsuspecting tourist presses one of those tempting buttons, I stumble and fall heavily on my knees, practically on my *face*: PROSTRATE before the Great Poet! Almost kiss the ground he walked on.

> I the poet William Yeats
> With old millboards and sea-green slates
> And smithy work from the Gort forge
> Restored this tower for my wife George.

Can't help feeling for that woman (and not just because her name was George), as I painfully negotiate the vertiginous staircase. Can't have been easy being Yeats's wife. Not on those STAIRS anyway. I spiral downwards, thinking of them in their cozy bed.

Saw Yeats's GHOST once. He must have one! BE one? Whatever. He was sitting on a Boston park bench looking straight at me: handsome, kindly, pleasant. He smiled on me beneficently! *Seemed* vaguely familiar, but I was in a hurry . . . Ah well, every poet has to spurn a poet's ghost at some point.

Biographical snippets continue to honk at me through his three-foot-thick walls as I limp down the lane, undone by crassness, old clothes upon old sticks to scare a bird.

Back at the hotel, I try to work. Find a curious passage in my late student's notebook, an outline for a screenplay or something. Kind of gives me the *creeps*, don't know why:

DISASTER MOVIE OUTLINE

VARIOUS CHARACTERS WITH CREDIT DIFFICULTIES, MARITAL PROBLEMS AND LOVESICKNESS, DESCEND ON IRISH HOTEL.

POSSIBILITY THEY WILL ALL BE <u>BOMBED</u> (OR ELSE BUY A LOT OF TRINKETS). THEY ALL NEED A SHAKE-UP!

OMINOUS SOUND OF SHELLS MASSING ON BEACH. WAVES HUFF AND PUFF. FREQUENT SHOTS IN SLO-MO OF LOW-FLYING WATER BIRDS.

CHARACTERS INCLUDE:
    The 3 Old Biddies
    The Smug Doctor
    The Smug Doctor's Wife
    The Smug Doctor's Smug Sons and Smug Daughter
    Owen (abject father of Ellen)
    Ellen (abject daughter of Owen)
    Ed (token madman)
    Hermit-woman
    Rogue Poet
    The Phantom Forms of the Children Rogue Poet Should Have
       Had

ELOÏSE

Connemara is Europe's most western point. I look out to sea in search of Massachusetts. We're lit by the same sun! But then I think of my beautiful handmade paper bag full of George's letters, to which no new ones have been added for years.

Lettershinna

Lettershanna

Lettermore

Lettercallow

Letterbeg

The wind and water of Connemara are telling me to move on, the ghosts of my parents quietly waiting, the Beatles tune in my head (let it be), the tides that push and pull me, the moon within me, the menstrual cramp that leads me back to the car (more Nurofen).

I am being watched. The kindly face of a donkey studies me. His feet are tied together, his legs worn bare by the rope, but he stumbles across the steep rocky yard to be spoken to.

The donkey's owner comes out of a nearby house. I mumble a question about the tied-up hooves. The man says the donkey is a rascal and would gallop out of his field if he wasn't tied. I nod and drive away, crushed by shyness, shame and guilt about the tender-faced donkey.

I go back to Clifden and call the RSPCA in Galway. They can get the donkey to a donkey sanctuary in Cork if I arrange for a vet to inspect him. Reluctantly, I call the local vet. He won't do anything because he knows the owner too well, but suggests I try to buy the donkey for £10 (the going rate for abused donkeys?).

I return to the cliff top, half-hoping the donkey will be gone or miraculously healed. But there he is, still hobbling. I knock on the door of the house. When the owner eventually answers, I offer to buy the donkey. Without a moment's pause, the man says I can have him for £100!

I baulk at letting this donkey-abuser profit from his cruelty. I baulk at bargaining him down. I baulk at spending £100! Oh, I just baulk and leave. Leave the poor donkey to his time-honoured fate.

For all I know it is one big *racket*, a dark sideline of the tourist trade. The vet makes a quick phone call to the owner, telling him a sucker is on her way to buy his donkey. The RSPCA's probably in on it too: as soon as one poor old donkey is shipped to Cork, another is put in its place to await a passing motorist's compassion.

Into the hotel bar to get a double whisky (weird, wind-blown, tear-stained woman seeking solace). Yet again I am confronted by the doctor who killed my parents, the man for whom I bow behind my menu, shuffle down corridors, hide in corners. I take the whisky up to my room, shunning the welcoming turf fires of all the world.

Connemara's radiating peninsulas and its islets broadcast in the ocean must have answered to the misanthropy of the sixth century, when every hermit wanted a desert to himself.

I was lying on my bed with the faint sounds of the wind and sea coming through the window and the hotel plumbing loudly whining through the walls, when the phone rang. I thought it might be the vet again about the donkey.

'Hello?' I said.

'Hello!' came a sprightly male voice (English). 'Remember me?'

'Uh, no . . .'

'We met today, in the hotel!'

The only person I'd nodded to that day was a man with a little girl.

'Don't you recognize my voice?'

(Had we even said 'hello'? – I couldn't remember.)

'Well, I'm not sure . . .'

'What are you *wearing*?'

'Uh . . . I'm sorry but . . . I've to go now.'

'You're not angry, are you?'

'Um, no, no, I just . . .'

'Can I call you again some time? I like talking to you.'

'Um, I have to go.'

'I'll call you later then.'

And he hung up. A pervert. In the hotel. That nice man with the nice little daughter?! But what did it matter? What did any of it matter, I thought, as I climbed drink-sodden into my brown bath.

THE DOCTOR'S WIFE

Again I find him in the bar, my husband, smiling, smiling. And I leave him to it, leave the children too to fend for themselves. I retreat to our room to play my complicated version of patience. With each card I slap him, my husband. May God destroy his house. I hear him talking still. May he die so I can rest.

He is Eden, the war criminal. A dog is better than him, the bastard, the donkey! May we have victory over him. Men! Their necks need to be broken. A woman should beat her husband daily. On his head, on his mouth so he can't speak!

God grant me victory over my husband. May I see him begging in the street. He never gives us anything. He used to give me money and butter, mangoes, peaches, watermelon. Now he doesn't give us anything.

> Bees that lie on their backs will often grasp and cling to a corner of the card if it be presented to them. The edge of the card may then be struck sharply against the rim of the jar, with the result that the bee falls into the killing-jar.

The doctor's wife, mother-to-be, twirls round and round the swimming pool, weeping slightly. She has just caught a glimpse of herself in a mirror, looking balloon-like. She recognizes that she will never again have her husband's love, nor that of any other man. She knows this clearly. No one could ever want to touch such a monstrosity.

She weeps as she swims, as she eats, as she sleeps. (Her children try not to notice.)

GEORGE

He toils not, neither does he sting.

Pretty cute place, Ireland. Nobody on the roads except sheep and unmarried sons, for whom life is a lot of wet walking. I like the little haystacks weighted down by white squares of cloth, with a stone at each corner. How to get *them* into my poem?

I should be WRITING it. Instead I'm touring literary sites! Don't know what's gotten into me. Even sites BARELY literary. Anything to get me out of the hotel and away from my DESK, well, table, a table with a drawer full of hotel stationery and local info: lists of LITERARY SITES TO VISIT.

Today I arranged a trip to an island, to see Beckett's great-uncle's granddaughter's house. Yeah, well, whoever, she sounded kind of nice on the phone when we were arranging the visit. In fact, I'd decided it was quite possible we'd get MARRIED. It wasn't love, I just want to live on an island.

She said she'd meet me on the shore and row me over. I observed a lot of brown water lapping against pebbles as I waited for her – pretty CALM considering I was about to meet my future BRIDE. Finally caught sight of a little blue rowboat about halfway across the lake. But where was my love? Eating potato chips and watching TV,

I guess. It was her HUSBAND in the boat, along with a pregnant dog.

When I did eventually meet the great writer's great-uncle's great granddaughter, she was even greater than I'd dared hope. I liked her. FAR TOO MUCH. The two of them showed me around the place, which had been built by Beckett's uncle to protect the family from the 'sorrowful civil war' as they movingly put it.

Yep, I still wanted to live there. But without the husband. I wanted to warm my would-be wife in bed in that big impractical summer house on winter nights, spoon position. I wanted to row across that little lake to get us groceries from the Rossadilly store. I wanted to be there when the dog had her puppies!

But then sanity returned (somewhat). I suddenly began to wonder what the hell I thought I was doing there, bothering Beckett's kinfolk with my neurotic musings, yearning degenerately to hump Beckett's uncle's granddaughter while at the same time trying to think up intelligent Beckett questions. I was at a considerable disadvantage *there*, since the only biographical detail I could remember about Beckett was that James Joyce's daughter was in love with him. Couples and their couplings PLAGUE me.

Longed to go but felt I had to make the hubby's two ROWBOAT trips worthwhile. Tried to entertain 'em! Thought they must need COMPANY, stuck out there on that little ISLAND all the time (why else had they opened it as a literary site?). But when they failed to offer me a drink, ran out of stuff to say about the Beckett clan and started jabbering about the bats in the attic, I knew it was time to go. Bats! I wanted PUPPIES.

151

Connemara, wilderness of gabbro,
Mica, mantle, schists and strata.
Pinched green marble malleable moonscape.
Lapping auburn water, licking
Undersides of rowboats, pickling
Ancient forests, peatbogs, poets.

Tourists come to buy their baubles,
Babbling bubbles of unmeant warmth.
Land of IRE, ire and enmity,
Open as an open wound.

ELOÏSE

January, 1881, I perceived a poor ant lying on her back and quite unable to move. The legs were in cramped attitudes, and the two antennae rolled up in spirals. She was, of course, altogether unable to feed herself. After this I kept my eye on her. Several times I tried uncovering the part of the nest where she was. The other ants soon carried her to the shaded part. On 4th March the ants were all out of the nest, probably for fresh air, and had collected together in a corner of the box; they had not, however, forgotten her, but had carried her with them... On 5th March she was still alive, but on the 15th, notwithstanding all their care, she was dead!

At the present time I have two other ants perfectly crippled in a similar manner, and quite unable to move, which have lived in two different nests ... the one for five the other for four months.

How can I account for my peculiar behaviour? I was lonely, isolated, a hunk of hankering humanity away from its normal routine. I was longing, in a general sort of way, for a *man*. This was no mere inconsequential longing. This was the kind that wakes you at dawn, scavenges for scraps all day, that broods like a bored child in the back seat and makes all of life a shuddering dissatisfaction. It was a great gathering wave that seemed to rise up out of the ground and carry everything before it, the grass, the trees, the rooftops, in a plaintive cry of FUCK ME!

But perhaps it was only the sound of birds wheeling across the wilderness of Connemara.

The most advanced virgin queens are soon allowed to gnaw their way out of their cells.

GEORGE

This hotel is weird. So sleepy . . . They all need a good SHAKE-UP.
I guess that's what the fucking Murder Weekend's for. Can't wait:
English tourists wallowing in death. (I plan to be OUT.)

It should *really*, should undoubtedly, be the perfect place for me
to work on my goddam poem. Nothing to disturb me except the
sound of ancient plumbing, and the voice of the ghastly DOCTOR
(it can be heard for miles). I have dutifully spent the day sequestered
in my room. I figure if I get BORED enough, I might just write
something.

> *See me take her, turn her, learn her,*
> *Searching for that pretty little*
> *Doorway . . .*

In the end I get SO bored I go down to the beach and there,
twiddling her feet in the gray pebbles like a sulky child (which she
is), is VENETIA, my patroness. And she's got NO HAIR. Jeez, she's
followed me.

Largest pet litters:

puppies – 23
kittens – 19
gerbils – 14
guinea pigs – 12
hamsters – 26
rabbits – 24
mice – 34

VENETIA

She stands before the window, the long white curtain billowing towards her legs. She bare. Even her head, which she's shaved.

She stands in a Connemara cottage feeling the breeze on her body. She wants to be all flesh. Hairless, thoughtless, nothing but flesh. Nothing. A trip to another land where she can be baseless, base. Where she can air her hairless flesh.

Through the billowing curtain she feels a brief moment of intense sunshine, and hears the dim rattle of dead leaves.

Flesh, all flesh. She walks around the cottage naked, maximizing the surface area of flesh, then returns to the bed where George is. He sleeps. Venetia has added his snores to the things that she loves on the bare face of the earth.

ELOÏSE

Birds that breed most early in these parts:

      Raven,

      Song-thrush,

      Blackbird,

      Rook,

      Woodlark,

      Ring-dove,

'What colour are your knickers?'

'Black.'

'What else are you wearing?'

'Why?'

'I'm trying to picture you.'

'Well, a skirt.'

He was still a little too interested in my clothing. But I liked his voice. And I was touched by the occasional glimpse I got of him wandering round the hotel with his daughter. Surrendering stoically to the hotel telephone, I talked to him for hours! I had hopes of rehabilitating him.

      Upper parts black.

      Upper parts black and white.

Upper parts grey.

Upper parts brown.

Upper parts green or greenish.

Upper parts blue.

Upper parts white.

Upper parts pink or pinkish.

Upper parts golden-yellow.

Upper parts red.

The telephone rings again. And again.

'Hello?'

'. . . What are you wearing?'

This is getting ridiculous. I implement Plan B.

'What would you *like* me to be wearing?' I say.

'Can I come and see you?'

'Only if you make *me* come.'

'Uh! Well, I'd like to do that . . .' says he.

'How?'

'Er, what?'

'How would you do it?'

'Well, um . . . Shove my willy up you?'

'What else?'

'Um, well, suck your, um . . . nipples?'

'Yes?'

'And uh, feel your bum.'

' . . . and then what?'

A gentle discussion. One of many, late at night, after two or three whiskies, sharing fantasies and reminiscences.

My pervert. When everyone in the world seems perverse, a pervert seems no worse.

> Underparts wholly black.
> Underparts not wholly black.

OWEN

Owen stamps about in the stable yard. The ride is late getting back. Ellen, he imagines, is lying on the beach with a broken neck, encircled by useless onlookers, while the horses plod about in the background munching salty shrubs. In another five minutes, they'll think of sending for help. Another fifteen minutes after that, some-one will appear at the hotel with the awful news and he'll have to act *surprised*. Whatever he does, though, people will think he's callous, casual – what sensible parent would let his daughter, who's only a beginner, go off on a horse with an untrained instructor? They canter across the beach, she told him after her first ride! In fact, she didn't even know if it was cantering or galloping, only that she'd almost fallen, and wanted to do it again.

Another worried parent has appeared, the pregnant woman. Owen smiles companionably at her, but actually hopes it's *her* child that has broken its neck. He looks up at the brow of the hill behind the stables, trying to identify the most likely spot for the ponies to appear, if they do return. At that moment a scream is heard, and Owen turns to see Ellen on an out-of-control pony speeding bumpily across a different field, closely followed by a horse carry-ing a whooping boy who seems to be trying to overtake. This is spurring Ellen's pony on. Ellen is frightened and crying.

Owen, nervous of horses and unsure of what to do, none the less moves forward, hoping he can catch hold of the bridle somehow as the pony clatters by. But as soon as the pony reaches the end of the field it slows down of its own accord and walks coolly into the stable yard, shaking its huge scary head. The pregnant woman is now yelling at her beastly boy for terrifying everybody. She has a strange accent and a hurt look in her eye. Owen warms to her. Poor woman. The kid is obnoxious! Now he's complaining that he wanted to ride Ellen's pony and his wouldn't trot.

Owen and Ellen hobble back to the hotel distraught. She says she couldn't stop her pony from copying the boy's, and the boy was determined to canter all the time. She had to hold on to the saddle for dear life. So, it is *almost* as Owen had feared.

In the afternoon, Owen and Ellen go by boat to Inishbofin Island for the Inishbofin Arts Festival (they've already had a good look round the Connemara Vegetable Show). The boat's tight schedule leaves them only an hour on Inishbofin: time enough to eat soup and watch one man in a tent *prepare* to put on a one-man play.

Then it's back to Cleggan on the helplessly heaving boat full of passengers licking ice creams, standing inside, out of the rain. Ellen stands outside at the helm, looking for dolphins. There are no dolphins, and the boat is bouncing alarmingly over the waves. Owen feels he must stand outside with Ellen, though he hates seeing the extreme proximity of the sea (being taller, he gets a much better view of this than she does).

By the time they reach land, the sun is out again, the sudden squall over, and the water by the dock, Owen notes with grudging admiration, is turquoise. But it's still too close.

They photograph horses, donkeys, sheep, cows and cute haystacks all the way back to the hotel.

THE 3 OLD BIDDIES

As an adult you become your own guardian. You berate yourself for past mistakes and promise to do better. You devote yourself to your future self's wants. You do its chores for it, tidy up so that your future self can find things later, avoid committing crimes which will land your future self in prison, pay bills so your future self will be adequately provided with heat and lighting, food and shelter. You try not to smoke so your future self won't get cancer, and try to avoid hangovers. You curb all your enthusiasms so your future self won't find it's got too many hobbies and meetings and appointments to cope with. You even turn on the electric blanket an hour before bed so that your future self will be cosy. So much effort on behalf of someone who does not yet, may never, and definitely eventually won't, exist!

The old biddies were past caring about the future. They had no time for aftermath worries, no interest in repercussions. They were tired of self-admonishment. They lived for the moment. They wanted a good time and they wanted it now! To the shop assistants of Connemara they were just grey-haired old ladies in search of all-wool socks, shamrock brooches and whisky samples. To the clerks of credit-card companies, however, they were con artists wanted for a string of frauds throughout the UK.

OWEN

I don't regret a minute that we've spent together. Your dimpled hands when tiny, your eyes from birth like a whale's. You should know that you are splendid.

Owen was watching Ellen make her way nervously from the women's changing room to the side of the arctic-temperature swimming pool (only a child could *stand* it, he thought, but then noticed the nice pregnant woman was in there too). He was awash with love looking at Ellen's legs walking. As long as he lived he would never forget any part of her or anything about her. He was hazy now about what exactly a two-year-old or a four-year-old or a five-year-old is like, but in Ellen's case it was all of a piece with her as she was now. The past, present and future all tied in with the sight of her now, moving in the sun, hair blowing: a daughter.

(A father.)

ELOÏSE

'Why don't we go for a walk?'

'Wellll . . .'

'Please?'

'I don't . . . know.'

'It wouldn't take long. I want to look at you!'

'I'm a little busy.'

'It's such a nice day. Just for a minute.'

Downstairs, Eloïse stood nervously by the cold fireplace wondering a) why they hadn't lit a fire, b) if he would bring his daughter (that might make things a little less awkward), and c) what was she getting herself into. She was not a viable female thing! What was she *playing* at, pretending to be capable of . . . sex?! She was a sham, a walking swindle.

But the nice-looking man with the daughter never turned up. A gnarled moustachioed fellow approached her. He was even more nervous than she (: extremely twitchy), but as soon as he spoke she recognized the voice. She had *misidentified* her pervert! Ed was as pink and puffy as the pumpkin he led her round the back of the kitchens to see. It was huge and sounded hollow. She had an irresistible urge to sit on it.

'There you go, Your Majesty,' said Ed, as she positioned herself carefully on this throne. 'Do you mind me calling you that? . . Your Majesty, I mean.'

'No, no . . .'

Ed got down on bended knee.

'You're my queen bee! I've been looking for a woman just like you . . . You're very attractive! I like the way you talk to me . . .'

'Well . . .'

'On the phone.'

'. . . It's been fun . . .'

'I want you!' said Ed, and flattened her across his pumpkin. She couldn't *move*: she was pressed awkwardly against the pumpkin's stalk and was fearful of struggling in case she reactivated her neck problem (though the feel of Ed's wiggly willy bumping against her leg was not pleasant).

'I need a *woman*,' he puffed in her ear.

'That's very noble,' she offered lamely, and was released.

Ed was undone, *ennobled!* He stood up, looking round, sheepishly chuffed.

'Well, I don't know about that . . .' Ed said.

'No, it *is* noble,' said Eloïse as she sat up, rubbing her back where the phallic stalk had been. 'Every man should devote himself to making one woman happy.'

'Hmmm, well, don't know as I've got time for *that!*'

'One happy woman is all.'

She got up, feeling like a battered Delphic oracle, and walked stiffly away. One happy woman indeed! She headed for her car – she could at least escape Ed for the afternoon that way. One happy woman is all.

ED

Unnerved by his encounter with Eloïse, Ed didn't at first know what to do with himself. So he played with his pumpkin and as he pumped he fumed – about the Connemara Vegetable Show. It had all been a terrible disappointment to him. Typical Paddies. They wouldn't know a good pumpkin if it jumped up and punched them in the gob!

Firstly, there was nowhere to put his pumpkin – no space had been allocated for it! They said it was too big. Too big? What were they on about? What's too big when you're talking giant pumpkins? It was a deflating thing for both Ed and his pumpkin to hear.

There was also no machinery available to move the thing from the van to the tent. Ed had to drag it himself, on a sheet, on his hands and knees across the gravel path, which bruised the pumpkin's underside. And in the end, it turned out that there was no prize that could be awarded to a giant pumpkin except 'Weirdest Vegetable' (which Ed naturally refused). They just weren't interested in giant pumpkins! All growing fucking shamrocks for the tourist trade, and decorative gourds. They didn't know their arse from their elbows, the Irish: Ed had found a mango on the Melon table, labelled 'Dwarf Melon'. Dwarf melon! Fucking idiots.

Ed had eventually flounced off with his pumpkin (not an easy thing to do with a vegetable that big), lugging it to the back door of the hotel kitchens where he'd presented it – with thudding irony

– to the chef. To make a pumpkin pie. Or, say, three hundred pumpkin pies! (So far, the chef hadn't taken him up on the offer.) After that, Ed had skulked round the hotel feeling cheated, occasionally peeing on the Connemara Vegetable tent at night. If he'd only brought the necessaries, he would have *bombed* the place. He could show these bloody Paddies a thing or two about bombs!

The Murder Weekend was the only thing he had to look forward to. That sounded a good lark.

On his way to pee on the tent again, he met Ellen. They got chatting, and got along so well that Ed snuck into the marquee and stole Ellen a pomegranate from the Exotic Vegetable display. The Irish can't even tell an exotic vegetable from an *erotic* vegetable! Fruit. Whatever.

Knowing she shouldn't accept gifts from strangers, Ellen (or Persephone, as she now privately called herself) skipped off to eat the pomegranate in the shade behind the stables.

Ed wandered off to the hotel, wondering if he might see Eloïse again there and whether he wanted to (she seemed a bit weird). Turning a corner in the long dark corridor, he came upon the more luscious Niamh, chambermaid of one's dreams, being groped by the doctor. Ed scuttled behind a pillar with a good view. The doctor was holding Niamh's hands behind her back, trying to kiss her. Ed wanted next go.

'Bugger off!' shouted Niamh. Escaping from his grasp with practised aplomb (and maybe a hint of martial arts training), she gave the estimable doctor a shove that nearly sent him into Ed's pillar. Quickly regaining his supposed dignity, the doctor pretended he was going in that direction anyway. Ed surreptitiously followed Niamh down the corridor until she managed to duck so swiftly through a doorway that she lost him. Traipsing back and forth, trying to figure out *which* door, occupied the rest of Ed's afternoon.

ELOÏSE

Nutmegs and Margin shells

Harps and spiny Whelks

Turrids

Volutes

Auger shells

Babylon shells

Cones

Still shaking from my encounter with the pumpkin man, I drive to the beach near Grandma's house. *My* beach where I used to take refuge from her whining, where I swam naked in little warm pools of water until Grandma found out and made me wear a suit.

It has been taken over by a hideous Scuba-Diving Centre. I look at the centre, then at the rough grey sea, and think, why not? No one could find me in twenty or thirty feet of water. I have watched my share of Jacques Cousteau films. The sea is a perfect place for hermits. No one would know I was there.

But it turns out I need a swimsuit, shorts, shampoo, and an *appointment*. I'm so rattled by this I can't decide whether to do it or not.

I creep back into the hotel and sit on my bed brooding about pumpkins, phone calls, appointments, Jacques Cousteau and my youthful notion of becoming a marine biologist, until I finally work up the courage to ring the scuba-diving centre and arrange a lesson for the next day.

Dread and despair all morning for *fear* of scuba-diving! When I get there, an intensely beautiful man tells me he's my Individual Instructor. He makes me sit in the tearoom and watch a video about scuba-diving, on which I will later be quizzed. Having fully grasped the video I am rather looking forward to the quiz. I also have to fill out a health form – if I answer Yes to any of the questions on it, I can't go scuba-diving. I answer Yes to three: ear trouble in childhood, neck trouble now, nausea. I can't go scuba-diving! I don't even get to do the scuba-diving *quiz*. What a swizz. Am offered snorkelling instead. I do not dare tell my handsome Individual Instructor how inferior I consider snorkelling to scuba-diving (would he be hurt or relieved?). I end up agreeing to snorkel.

The terrible embarrassments connected with the 'dry-suit'. The first one he gives me is too small. I can only get into three-quarters of it. Still in the suit and almost in tears, I have to pad past all the lounging scuba-divers in the tearoom to ask my instructor for a bigger one. I plod back upstairs. The bigger suit fits, *sort* of, but I've wrenched my shoulder so badly getting into the first, I can only pull this one on halfway! I plod downstairs again. Through the tearoom. This time, several hostile scuba-divers have a very good look at me not looking too good in my dry-suit.

My instructor takes me in hand in a room full of the vaguely human forms of dry- and wet-suits hanging from above, drained and crumpled forms all in a line. He tells me to lift my arms. I lift them cooperatively, but he meant the arms of my *suit*. Into these he flicks baby powder, which is supposed to help ease my arms into the sleeves.

I duly stick my head and arms into the suit and now can hardly *breathe*: the suit is cutting off my circulation and strangling me! The only things that fit comfortably are the gloves, but he does them up so tight that they hurt too. The underwater world will have to be pretty spectacular to make up for this. But then – miraculously – after a momentary absence my instructor reappears in *his* dry-suit, which is *sleeveless*. Forearms in full view. I lust. We tramp down to the sea.

There is much physical contact necessary between a novice snorkeller and her Individual Instructor. One could easily misconstrue his intentions, the way he binds and straps my chest and sticks my flippers on my feet, then leans lightly on me while he puts on his own. Next he carefully teaches me how to blow up my buoyancy vest which sits on top of a huge weighted belt round my waist (things have not moved on much from Jules Verne), and forces my hat over my head.

With the hat on, I can't breathe, and we're not even in the water yet. It also mushes up my face in a manner that deeply worries me. Pink, puckered and choking, I long already to be back in civilization, with lipstick and hair and a tissue for my nose, safe and loveless on dry land, but first I must enter the sea with this handsome man who feels nothing for me. I am in fact utterly miserable. Misled by Jacques Cousteau.

My instructor makes me kneel down and practise breathing underwater. I immediately fall over and flounder there like a beetle on its back. I smile bravely, pretending I'm having a good time, try to regain my feet but *can't*: I am a big helpless inflatable blob, bobbing in one or two feet of water.

Eventually we swim out a little. I try to snorkel. Water keeps getting up my nose. Each time it does, I'm supposed to turn over and float on my back while I readjust my snorkel and catch my breath. My Individual Instructor waits, fairly patiently (he's getting paid 17 Irish punts after all, whether or not I ever manage to see the wonders of the underwater world). When we are finally swimming again, he tells me to look down. I do, and the first thing I see, right under me, about six feet down, is a shark! Terror. Panic. I start choking again. I want to swim away but instead have to lie on my back *choking*, salt water in every orifice and about to be mauled by a shark.

My instructor waits. When I've recovered somewhat, he asks if I noticed the *dogfish*: totally harmless and about four feet long (it looked *ten* to me – the mask magnifies everything). But it makes no difference. I've realized I am in the same element as *monsters*, and they could *eat* me.

My instructor keeps diving down to the bottom and bringing things up to show me. As if I care. A sea urchin – one side the eye, the other the mouth, as far as I can understand it. Hermit crabs. I am incapable of mastering the 'OK' sign he seems to like to use underwater (thumb and forefinger forming a circle). Whenever he does it at me, I *nod* – which makes me splutter and choke. *Not* OK. Not OK at all! He shows me a starfish, one leg smaller than the others: a *replacement* leg (ugh). Spider crab. Some sort of flat fish on the bottom, burrowing under the sand (what a life). But worst of all are the high wavering cliffs all round us, covered with seaweed fronds. It is all too deep, too deep.

Nose full of salt water, choking steadily, I am desperate to get *out*, but would rather drown than admit this to my instructor: my lust for him is now the only thing keeping me *alive*. Or human. The rest of me is but a spluttering, runny-nosed, bulbous thing (new kind of sea monster).

I can barely walk when I'm finally allowed out of the water. I'm panting, smothered by my own suit. I'll breathe *later*, I promise myself, pretending to be able to walk.

Final humiliation back in the rubber-suit room: my instructor has to pull the suit *off* me, thereby getting a glimpse of my damp-rotty old shorts before we're both submerged in the rancid smell of the suit. I wash my hair upstairs, splashing cold water on my face to try to reduce its incredible pinkness (caused by forty-five minutes of near-strangulation), then go down to meet him in the tearoom. We drink some tea together. I'm so relieved to be on dry land, I say I *enjoyed* my snorkelling lesson, even hint I might want to do it again sometime! But he's not listening to my lies. He's got his diary out, already thinking about the next underworld experience he can inflict on somebody else.

GEORGE

Individual: Watch the puck
Individual: Talk it over
Individual: Get up on the play
Individual: Positional factor
Individual: Be aggressive
Individual: If you're not clicking
Individual: Giving credit
Individual: When to pass
Individual: When you pass, break!
Individual: If the ice is slow
Individual: Get off if tired
Individual: Fundamental offence
Individual: Missed goals

I am coming apart here! Ireland has made a meal of me. It's eating me ALIVE. Hungry kind of place.

Or is it just Venetia? She's after my SOUL. Seems to find this sort of cannibalism romantic!

> *Empty Connemara moonscape –*
> *Long-gone, those who should still BE here.*
> *Vessels fueled by English apathy*

Took the helpless hapless poor to
Strange new wastelands. There my starving
Homeless, homesick forebears started
Families — little knowing someday
One would be a skater, back upon a
Bright-lit neon moonscape.

For the Crazy Irish 'love of conflict'
Carried down the line to ME. Not just on
Ice my civil disobedience, but
In my wrongful negligence, my 'duty'.
DEATH and WASTE my only offspring.

Tender haystacks fuchsias, peatland.
Peasants who have never married;
Life but a business of wet walking,
Soft rain, a cow or sheep to visit.
Wrath and reason have no place here.
No place, no USE, for my confusion,
Chaos, conflict. Nor my coldness.

1. INT. Venetia's rented holiday cottage — late afternoon.

VENETIA, DRESSED, IS TRYING TO LUG GEORGE (NAKED SPONGING IRRESOLUTE LOUSE) OUT OF BED. THE LOUSE DOES NOT WANT TO BE AWAKE. IF AWAKE, HE WILL HAVE TO ACKNOWLEDGE (NOT FOR THE FIRST TIME) THAT HE HAS SOMEHOW SUCCUMBED TO SERVICING HIS PATRONESS! HE IS NO LONGER CONVINCED THIS WHOLE TRIP TO IRELAND WAS A GOOD IDEA.

CUT TO AMAZING BLUEY CLOUDS FORMING OVER GLOWY BLOWY HILLS.

VENETIA

(coquettishly)

Come on! Up. We've got to get to the hotel.

GEORGE

Why the hell do we have to go there?

VENETIA

The Murder Weekend! Have you
forgotten the Murder Weekend??

GEORGE

Goofy Brits pretending to be Colonel
Mustard or Miss Scarlet? Gimme a BREAK!

VENETIA

(genuinely startled)

But . . . I thought that's what you came for!

GEORGE

I came to write my POEM.

VENETIA

Oh, but I so wanted you to try it.

2. INT/EXT. Venetia's rented car – a few minutes later.

GEORGE

(sullenly)

Cute place, Ireland. You know, Venetia, the
fact is, Venetia, I don't *go* for murder

mysteries, thrillers, detectives, forensics. I
happen to think it's kind of sick to take such
a prurient interest in death! It's OBSCENE.
Death really ISN'T that entertaining!

VENETIA (V. O.)
Our first argument! How thrilling.

CAR PASSES LONE DONKEY IN FIELD. CLOSE-UP OF DONKEY'S FEET:
THEY ARE TIED TOGETHER WITH ROPE THAT HAS WORN BARE
PATCHES ON ITS FETLOCKS. THE HOOVES ARE CRACKED AND SPLAYED.

CUT TO DISTANT SHOT OF VENETIA'S CAR ZOOMING ALONG.

3. INT. Rossadilly Hotel lounge – that night.
NIAMH THE CHAMBERMAID IS READING ALOUD FROM THE LITTLE
BOOKLET THAT CAME WITH THE HOTEL-GUIDE-TO-MURDER-WEEK-
ENDS KIT.

NIAMH
It is June 1940, in Paris. The Germans are
about to enter the city. The trains are full,
the roads to the south a hopeless snarl--

GEORGE
(interrupting)
Jesus, the whole thing's stolen
from *Casablanca*!

NIAMH
(not hearing him)
An anonymous letter arrives, offering

177

each of you a ticket on a government
train heading for the relative safety of
southern France.

GEORGE
(mumbling)
Yeah, and you'll REGRET it. Maybe not
today, maybe not tomorrow, but soon
and for the rest of your life . . .

GENERAL CONSTERNATION IN THE LOUNGE. EVERYONE FROWNS AT
GEORGE. NIAMH CONTINUES.

NIAMH
During the trip, murder is discovered!
The passengers must decide who among
them has committed the crime.

VENETIA GASPS APPRECIATIVELY. THE 3 OLD BIDDIES SQUEAL WITH
DELIGHT. DOCTOR NODS CONSPIRATORIALLY AT NIAMH, WHO IGNORES
HIM.

NIAMH IS LONGING FOR GALWAY.

PEOPLE SCATTER, COLLECTING THEIR SCRIPTS, COSTUMES AND VICTIM-
OR-MURDERER CARDS. GEORGE JUST SITS THERE, LOOKING MOROSELY
INTO HIS GLASS. VENETIA STANDS OVER HIM, PATTING HIS HEAD
HAPPILY.

CLOSE-UP OF GEORGE LOOKING GLOOMILY INTO GLASS.

CUT TO PHOTOS OF LAP DOGS:

        CHIHUAHUA

        PEKINESE

        SHIH–TZU

        PUG

        TOY POODLE

        YORKSHIRE TERRIER

        BRUSSELS GRIFFON

ELOÏSE

Ingratitude, thou marble-hearted fiend,
More hideous, when thou show'st thee in a child,
Than the sea-monster.

The guilt of inheritance. I hated the woman. *I don't deserve her house.* I expected it to have disintegrated beyond repair since her death, thereby rightly disinheriting me. But there it is, looking down from its old secluded spot above Lough Muck, just as Grandma used to (we secretly called her Lady Muck). The garden has been invaded by sheep. Some lie serenely by the little brook. But the house seems intact and defiant, that single sour storey of stone. I open it with a key and a kick.

Depression of a place too long deprived of? electricity? love? Musty books, beds, those blankets that never kept out the cold, the three now-silent clocks. Dead bugs on the grey painted cement floor of the hall. Otherwise no sign of life or death. Dank ugly formicaed kitchen and, on closer inspection, something new to me: two separate loos, right *next door* to each other. The whole of the back end of the house has been given over to defecation! Improvements only an old woman would make.

Holding an old book on bees snatched from off a shelf, I sit for hours in the front parlour, in the dowdy dimness, incapable of movement, the victim of snorkelling and other old mistakes. There is nothing left of Grandma in that house, no smell, no stink, no sign, no ghost. But she can still reduce me to torpor and grief.

I can't live here.

What finally galvanizes me is the thought of banknotes! My father told me once that Grandma hid banknotes behind the wallpaper (old refugee habit). I get up and start pessimistically feeling the walls, unable to believe that Grandma would leave me anything so *useful*. I look behind the turned-up corners of the wallpaper in the hall, feel along the bedroom walls for tell-tale bumps, pursue my chosen profession: inheritance.

It is in her bedroom that I finally find something, but it's not banknotes. When I pull at a strip of bubbly buckled wallpaper, they cascade to the floor, tiny pieces of paper covered with Grandma's scribblings. Poetry!? How my heart sinks at the sight.

The downside of inheritance: I must *read* them. I stuff all I can find into carrier bags (even the kitchen of a dead woman is encumbered with plastic bags), and drive carelessly and gloom-laden back to the hotel.

Miss Clavel ran fast and faster
To the scene of the disaster.

GEORGE

Nothing graceful in this gliding . . .

I watch the murdering from afar: poets do not take part in Murder Weekends (not if they can *help* it anyway). The other guests don't seem all that absorbed either. Venetia's the most avid, AVIDITY being her THING. Everybody goes around investigating things, talking to each other like 1940s BBC announcers (oh, death's SO genteel), but as soon as they get a crime-free hour they're all in the bar glugging it down for all they're worth. Then another corpse is found and off they trudge, slightly sozzled sleuths, to round up the usual suspects.

I cower in an armchair by the fire, hoping not to be detected there, safely encased as I am in self-disgust. I feel a bit like I felt the night my wife, sitting in the bleachers, got hit in the chest by a puck. She couldn't BREATHE for a while (neither could I). Wretched game, wretched as life itself.

How COULD I be SERVICING my PATRONESS? Whom I don't even LIKE. Who has no HAIR. God, the rich never give you a break. I should've known there'd be a catch somewhere. She probably has AIDS. And I deserve to get it. Have I NO CONTROL OVER MY DESIRES? Just a jerk who wants to get laid?

I sit in the lounge trying to get SHIT-FACED, downing Guinness and whisky by turns, comfy almost on my familiar cushions of confusion and regret – if it weren't for the sound of the dogged doctor chatting somebody up in the bar next door. His yelps bounce right off the intended prey and get ricocheted MY way. I could KILL that guy!

Then someone comes in the front door. INCREDIBLY SLOWLY. The consequent gust of wind nearly knocks my drinks off the fireguard. I turn ill-humoredly to see who the fuck is causing the tornado, and there's this misshapen maladroit milkmaid carrying in a load of bags, *backwards*. When she turns, I realize it's Eloïse.

I jump up, swaying somewhat but alert. Think a hug might be appropriate. APPROPRIATE?! The guy's been pining for this mythical creature for SIX YEARS and now he can't think of anything to say! Kind of like meeting a long-lost pal UNDER-WATER – you want to speak but it would come out all BUBBLES. She tolerates my hug – like a petrified tree would tolerate it – blushes, stumbles and is gone.

I sink back into my chair. It is as if a whole lifetime's confusion has been massing for this moment. What the FUCK am I going to do now? She's *here*, she's alive ... Of all the gin joints in all the towns in all the world, she walks into mine.

And the image comes back to me – can't get rid of it! – the image that made me leave my marriage, leave America, made me write about a mile's worth of poetry then somehow stopped me in my tracks with a brand of purposelessness all my own: Eloïse, tender and serious, opening her legs to me in that Marblehead hotel. Sailboats out in the bay, my thumb in her mouth, her hand on my jaw.

I MUST HAVE HER.

ELOÏSE

Is he staying in the *hotel*? *What* is he *doing* here? I must leave tomorrow. Tomorrow? I can't live until tomorrow. His power to *destroy* me. Again and again he hurts me! It is agony to see him.

I thought he would never touch me again, never touch me again.

Eloïse's grandmother's love poems went unread that night. But one person's sadness is much like another's: Eloïse had already inherited all her grandmother's despair.

She looks at the five packets of Nurofen in the bathroom. How had she had the prescience to buy so many? Time to take them *all*. (Suicide on Special Offer today!) She gets in bed with the Nurofen and a glass of water, hardly able to *breathe*. This is not just the effects of snorkelling. Her heart is broken. She weeps until she sleeps (and forgets to kill herself).

She dreams of wandering through a disused warehouse that has been polished and turned into a tourist sight. Dark blood-red cobblestones and shadows, cheery tourists striding by, and Eloïse lost. She cannot find the way out. *Barren womb and me alone.* A dream an old woman might dream. She wakes with a headache (ah, Nurofen) and blood running down between her legs. What a bloody mess the whole world is.

But she has a plan. She feels she will survive this day if she just takes it step by step and concentrates on purely practical things. She must pack. On her way into breakfast, she will ask the receptionist to prepare her bill. After breakfast, she will pay, then collect her bags and leave. Like an old woman might leave. Go to Grandma's. No one will ever find her there. There she can hide.

It will all be all be *all* be all right if she just takes it one step at a time. No one need know how terrified she is. But seeing George again is like meeting your own murderer in the afterlife. His power to destroy her.

As she packs, she scolds herself. *My own fault if he hurt me. He never asked me to love him.*

> We, the spectators of the upheaval, were now menaced by a great peril, and before us stood a terrible and inevitable death. All that the most active imagination could evoke, all that the most fertile mind could conceive, was far, far remote from the horrible, frightful situation in which we found ourselves.

At breakfast in the low-ceilinged dining room (another womb-room) – the last time I will ever sit here – the air is full of porridge, kippers and conflict, memories of childhood, sausages, orange juice and married people plump with pride and pity, all thinking that marriage somehow makes them more substantial beings, perhaps even *immortal*. The creepy doctor and his wife! Compared to them I am an insect, a parasite, licking up food which could be put to better use by People Who Run A Household.

If someone loved me I might be a nice placid sort of person, I meekly think to myself, before catching sight of George far away across the room. He doesn't see me: he's totally absorbed in talking to a beautiful woman in a big hat. *Do not speak to me, do not speak to me.*

I rush out of the room, out of the hotel, seek refuge on the rocky beach. The wind clasps me, then pushes me away, tired after a night spent sweeping and dusting the wilderness of Connemara. My feet sink in the round stones as I weep outrageously for my poet. But just as my moans reach a peak of plaintiveness they turn into loud guffaws! I am overwhelmed by the certainty that no one loves me, yet, insanely, this now seems a firm basis on which to build a life! I'm bathed in it, clasped by it: the apathy of the earth has *been* mine, and will *remain* mine, for ever. It is laid at my feet.

In short, I am nothing but a slug in the corner, not even worth crying for.

Etesian wind
Mistral
Chinook
Harmattan
Pampero
Monsoon
Kamsin
Sirocco
Doldrums

GEORGE

There is BIG STUFF, big stuff to FEEL that
No one tells you, no one CAN tell you.
Stuff you'd kill for, DIE for,
Stuff that you were BORN for.

When we first met, all those years ago, I felt her succumb to me so swiftly it almost hurt. It seemed too simple, too OBVIOUS. I didn't believe life could BE that simple. For me she tightened herself willingly into a ball. I felt dutybound to UNTWIST her, soothe and smooth her. Release her. In this I failed: I could not persuade her not to love me.

A love affair is an art form, creating something from nothing. How could I not see the beauty of the thing she had made for me?

Having as delicately as possible over bony breakfast kippers extricated myself from Venetia's clutches (*for ever*), I searched the hotel grounds for Eloïse (in between whiskies for me nerves). Finally I found her wandering near the stables. I was almost too drunk by this time to STAND UP but none the less boldly planted myself in front of her, blocking her path. She did not look at me. She was staring into the darkness of one of the stables.

'There used to be puppies here,' she muttered faintly.

'Eloïse.' The over-arching word.

Holding her hand, I ran with her back to the hotel, catapulting her past madmen and murderers, along the dark corridors, to the sanctity of my sunlit room. There, her panting began, wave upon wave of it. All the rhythms of the sea and its wildness.

Music is LOVE and LUST and SADNESS, the best sounds in the world, however repetitive they might be!

ELOÏSE

He came to rescue me! I could almost see my way through the maze as he took my hand and ran with me.

He sucked at my dried-out nipples, put his fingers in my atrophied cunt, lay across my barren back, encircled me. I clutched the quilt with wind-dried hands and kissed his shoulder with my bitter lips.

Slowly he touched me, slowly he turned me, moulding me into what he wanted until I was screaming and crying, how I loved him! and still he held me, like a lighthouse he would lead me, never leave me, like the Rock of Gibraltar he would heave me, rock me, ream me, until my six years half-alive worked themselves into a torrent of wanting and having. And being.

At last he would let me love him.

> ...A three-mile thick layer of basic rock, gabbro, coming up molten from deep in the earth's mantle, had been forced between its strata. As the two continents now moved towards each other, squeezing Japetus out of geography, the rim of the northern one was crumpled into long ridges ... In this upheaval proto-Connemara's rocks were repeatedly folded, faulted and thrust to and fro, until it became completely

detached and was driven eastwards by the oblique collision of the two landmasses. As the two halves of Ireland were finally rammed together, proto-Connemara was slid southwards over volcanic rocks of the southern shore of Japetus, and welded into its present position.

THE EARTH

The earth has embarrassing incidents of its own that keep it humble. It is not in total control of itself. It must make the most of gravity, tides, eruptions, winds and weather. The sun and moon too have some say. At any given moment on the earth an unforgiving river of molten lava, orange against a twilight sky, clots like menstrual blood as it stretches down a mountainside.

Life itself is as senseless and unthinking as the sea, as storms that finger prairies in spirals. In this it reflects the apathy of galaxies. We try to impose some purpose (love?) on life but through the fence we get glimpses of meaninglessness. When a pair of drowned children, brother and sister, wash up on a Norfolk beach and life just goes on. When generation after generation of donkeys suffer.

The map of the world is covered by layer upon layer of such tragedy. A body is always washing up on some shore.

There's no excuse for human existence, since we don't make honey! What have we got to offer the universe? The occasional unsolicited kindness, and the smiles of children. *This*, our only contribution, not love. What a disappointment, huh? We've all been cheated.

CAN YOU LOVE US? To embrace your species you must be the Nazi *and* the Jew, man and woman, the burglar and the burgled, colonizer, colonized – simultaneously. You must embrace your present and your past, embrace all the cruelty, the arrogance, the damn-fool mistakes, the Industrial Revolution! You must hold all this in your hand.

You can't? Then you cannot accept your species and will never be more than superficially content. You will never more than superficially *love*.

But even bees fail in this.

... According to my impression there are at least 2–3 million men and women well fit for work among the approx. 10 million European Jews. In consideration of the exceptional difficulties posed for us by the question of labor, I am of the opinion that these 2–3 million should in any case be taken out and kept alive. Of course this can only be done if they are at the same time rendered incapable of reproduction. I reported to you about a year ago that persons under my instruction have completed the necessary experiments for this purpose. I wish to bring up these facts again. The type of sterilization which is normally carried out on persons with genetic disease is out of the question in this case, as it takes too much time and is expensive. Castration by means of X-rays, however, is not only relatively cheap, but can be carried out on many thousands in a very short time. I believe that it has become unimportant at the present time whether those affected will then in the course of a few weeks or months realize by the effects that they are castrated ...

THE HOTEL CROWD

Ed has retreated from the Murder Weekend. No one seems to want to listen to a word he has to say about the possible culprit! He prefers to be in the kitchens bothering the chef.

'Fifty-three-pound beetroot I had once,' he says. 'Now what would you have done with that?'

The chef tries to think of an answer that isn't obscene.

'Well, I suppose . . . borscht?'

'And how about a seven-pound twelve-ounce tomato? Grew by mistake! One single tomato! It grew by mistake!'

Ellen is meditatively picking mussels off boulders. As he watches her beat her fist against the rocks, Owen allows himself a moment of pure joy. I don't regret a minute that I've spent with you . . . But then he remembers there is something inconsolable about Ellen, and this quells him. Her sorrow for her mother, he supposes, is unappeasable.

Niamh is very disappointed. Germans have invaded Paris, five different corpses have been provided, fifteen clues, lots of weapons, umpteen motives handed round on screwed-up pieces of paper — yet none of the guests could be bothered to figure out who was *responsible*. Daft things. She can't be doing with them.

And now the lecherous leprechaun of a doctor is coming her way. Probably to complain about the bloody boggy golf course again, or to feel her up.

'My wife!' he yells at Niamh.

'I'm not your wife, and wouldn't want to be!' retorts Niamh scornfully.

'No, it's ... she's having the *baby*!'

Niamh runs after him to the terrace, where she finds his wife lying on the warm flagstones with her legs shooting weirdly out in all directions. She's a monstrosity, poor thing, thinks Niamh as she kneels down and takes her hand.

'Can't you *do* something?' asks the doctor.

'You're the bloody doctor!' shouts Niamh, but she gets up quickly and heads for the phone. Already she regrets snapping at him: seeing him there, so worried about his wife, she wonders if she shouldn't have obliged him after all, one of those times in the corridor. Where's the harm?

The doctor, less concerned by his wife's predicament than by the hideousness she displays in it, is fascinated to note that, even in the midst of the imminent expulsion of his next child into the world, he can still be absorbed by the sight of Niamh's white riding breeches as she flaps off to the phone.

As it departs with the smug doctor, the smug doctor's wife, the smug doctor's smug sons and smug daughter and the smug doctor's as yet unborn, the ambulance has to squeeze past a garda van coming the other way.

A garda van full of old geezers, come to collect their wives, save them from a life of crime. But the 3 old biddies aren't at the hotel. Gone into Clifden to do some last bits of shopping.

Ridiculous hubbies in a temper.

Ed looks down at the hotel from far above, exhausted from his hike up the mountain and rather surprised to find it's as soggy at the top as it was at the bottom.

He watches the ambulance as he catches his breath. Who could be ill? He considers. Then, who would I *want* it to be? Probably some woman, not sure which. By now he's spent hours on the phone with almost every woman in the hotel. Part pleasure, part pain: his *duty* to express himself.

He resumes his march through bracken and bog. With each footfall he crushes an infant stream. Water gurgles at him making him want to pee – which he does, frequently, territorizing the whole bluff.

He has a walker's map and has informed the receptionist at the hotel of his intended route. But he feels alone and far away. Unaided and unloved. What would happen if he lost a shoe in this treacherous bog, broke an ankle, had a heart attack? Would they come for him, would they get an ambulance for *him*?

He looks down at tiny farmhouses. Then at the crazy array of clouds that hangs like an old frayed harness across the sky holding everything together, and at that moment the sky *moves*. Ed distinctly sees it shift a little. And again! He loses his footing and ends up perched on a damp, spiky bump of grass. Under him the earth is moving. The ancient buffeted bluff beneath him comes apart, bracken torn asunder by fissures a foot wide. When Ed leans over to look into a crack, he sees the molten magma of the earth.

The earth is so quiet, so reluctant to offend. What if it merely felt like *breathing*? What if it were merely to swell and, out of the blue, to sigh? The diaphragm opens, the ribs crack with disuse, air rushes in where angels fear to tread: an earthquake.

On the beach, Ellen and Owen feel nothing, but he says to her, 'Look! Look how low the tide is! I can barely see the sea.'

'See . . . sea?' Ellen chastises. She hates repetition.

The 3 old biddies gather up their cassette tapes of Irish folk songs, their tiny mugs bearing reliefs of Irish thatched cottages, their pinstriped Irish flannel Old Grandfather nightshirts. Time to be going, girls.

Suddenly, the whole shop rocks. It trembles. Hideous Waterford crystal smashes on the floor. In the havoc that follows, one cunning old biddy manages to swipe another tea towel and a tweed cap as a present for her old man.

ELOÏSE

It is a time of contentment. The fragrance of thousands upon thousands of blossoms will surround the hives, each still evening. This scent will come from the volatile, essential oils, collected with the nectar. It is perhaps the most beautiful time the bee-keeper will ever know.

Sun and shade caress the hillside, criss-crossing patterns intertwine on the water of the lake. I watch a surge of white exultant cloud, like the spurt of his semen in my throat. The staccato sounds of sex: cunt, cock, lick, suck, kiss, bite. Every noise is deafening, every sound is good. The world is beautiful, and it's being beautiful just for me. I never knew it held such miracles as this within its crevices. *He has come back to me, he has come back to me.*

He is everything to me, his hands the only hands, his voice the only voice. I open the window to breathe in the wind and waves. A goose flies over the water and my hopes soar. Maybe it is not too late, *too late*. But waves of anger, sadness, lust and hate rage within me. How could he have left me? He will leave me again. He will disappear.

I turn to him on the bed. He *must* be real – he's wearing a white T-shirt! *He has come back to me*: the one death that could be reversed.

I go to him, I *will* be with him, as long as he will let me, my fingers on his chest, his thighs, his cock, his lips — my new bag of worldly possessions. And we will cry together, for he has *saved* me, saved me from the underworld.

If only life could stop right now, so we never have to leave this room, never have to think again about the future or the past. You are the wind and the sea and the ground beneath me. You are *everything*.

If only it could all end now.

Thus, in her ecstasy, Eloïse dreams of apocalypse. Unable to save the world, she toys with its destruction.

This, our inheritance.

THE EARTH

No one expected the tidal wave that followed the earthquake, except the dolphins who swam way out to sea. But to them it was merely a big wave. Dolphins know that water runs through everything. It covers seven-tenths of the earth. It cannot be ignored.

The Dutch fight it non-stop, they stole their onion fields from it, their tulips. But the sea will have Holland back in the end. Its placidity deceives. You expect it to be benevolent? It holds more horrors than the human mind, or love. It is a monster, mammoth and uncontrollable and, like love, has its own unfathomable time-scale.

Whales beached themselves along the coast of Connemara, caught off guard by the low tide. They waited for the unreliable sea to come back and fetch them, their helpless bodies aching in the weakly enfolding breeze.

Sheep and creamy-coloured milk cows fell fretfully through cracks left by the earthquake as they made instinctively for the hill-tops. There was a flocking of crows, had anyone bothered to look, and much barking of dogs. But people were too busy brushing up the broken crockery (housework to the last) and checking damage to walls and ceilings. They were unaware for a while of the wave, coming fast now to sweep them all away.

It moved with ease across the beach, across the fields. It deposited fish in the fuchsia hedges along its path as it thundered unthinking towards the peatbogs (which welcomed it, being kin). A ten-foot-high milky-green wave surged up the cosy riverbed behind some cottages. People in the gardens had time to yell at each other to run away but they couldn't escape it, and as they were consumed they yelled for their mothers instead.

Abused donkeys and cute haystacks, woolly jumpers, bombs and insurrection, sheets of accordion music, young scholars from the local schools, cars from the scrap heaps and coffins from the cemetery, all floated off to less shallow graves.

It is only the sea, it doesn't have malice, it is merely itself, has to be. Swim *under* and you'll survive, swim *away* from rocky ledges and houses, boats and cars and land and jobs and towns and life itself and you will be all right.

Or so thinks Owen, as he swims, with his daughter clinging to his shirt. She trusts him, this forceful father pounding through the waves. He would not let her drown. Children do not die with their *parents*.

But he has long since given up any real hope of surviving. Instead he pedantically coaches her (his paternal duties the last thing to dissolve), commenting on the surreal debris that floats with them, articles from land. They come upon a little island – a two-foot-square pad of earth bobbing like a jellyfish – on which grows a sprig of lavender.

'That's lavender,' he tells her.

But she doesn't bother listening. He always repeats himself. He will tell her again some time what lavender is, and she'll attend to it then. In fact he says they might come back and get some lavender later.

Owen and Persephone paddle away from all trace of land, he keeping her as calm as possible. But in the end father and daughter will rest their heads on the warm breast of the wave – mother of all mistakes – and sink.

Others, riding the swell, spinning round in eddies, swallowed up repeatedly and then spat out again, slide through the murk of their existences and out to sea. Hoping to save themselves, they stay awake, stay alive and afloat, for as long as they can. One old woman, limbs broken, hangs from a treetop by her *teeth* until she's too tired. No one to help her.

Round her swims a shoal of naked children, blue as dolphins in the pale green sea. The children, the old, the sick: Connemara hands over its valuables.

The 44 elements in sea water (besides oxygen and hydrogen),
in order of abundance:

Chlorine
Sodium
Magnesium
Sulphur
Calcium
Potassium
Bromine
Carbon
Strontium

Boron

Silicon

Fluorine

Nitrogen

Aluminum

Rubidium

Lithium

Phosphorus

Barium

Iodine

Arsenic

Iron

Manganese

Copper

Zinc

Lead

Selenium

Cesium

Uranium

Molybdenum

Thorium

Cerium

Silver

Vanadium

Lanthanum

Yttrium

Nickel

Scandium

Gold

Mercury

Radium

Cadmium

Chromium

Cobalt

Tin

The hotel became a breakfast nook for fish that liked porridge. And its former guests? The old biddies were washed out of the souvenir shop and the world, still clutching postcards they'd never paid for and now would never write on. Niamh, drenched and crying on a roof but still luscious, was rescued by some fishermen, though in general it was each man for himself and most of the survivors were young and male.

The smug doctor escaped annihilation, as smug doctors so often do, but his family succumbed, *one* before he had even drawn his first breath, which made this infant one of the few to perish without swallowing their tongues in terror.

Eloïse was dragged from George's arms and engulfed in darkness. The wave came upon her so fast she had no time to realize she was breathing water, not air. Her bloated body eventually washed up on some shore. It was by then an empty vessel full of gases, a bottle that didn't look like a bottle. As we all are.

George could do nothing himself but plunge through darkness on the rivering wave, above and below and inside it by turns. He survived by thinking about Gary, Indiana, the ugliest city in the world, a city piled high with tyres! He sang to himself the cloying annoying song he'd sung as a bored kid on long car journeys: 'Gary Indiana Gary Indiana Gary Indiana!' It gave him hope: if even the thought of GARY, INDIANA would do, he must want to live.

After the deluge, he returned to London bereaved. After all his hesitations, he knew now that he had loved Eloïse, and wasted her. (He had her cats to remind him, rescued from their two-cat chalet at the cattery.)

> *All was tending mending kindness*
> *Making up for time lost, making*
> *Love to last a lifetime, making*
> *NONSENSE of my THEORIES.*

His epic poem had been washed away in the maelstrom, and disappeared again pretty quickly after he rewrote and published it (a few hundred copies sold). But its mere existence greatly added to George's sex appeal (which after all is why men write poetry), and thus enabled him to carry out the important task he'd set himself in Eloïse's memory: to fuck the wasted women of England. SOMEBODY HAD TO DO IT.

And Ed, the man of the moment, the man *on the scene*, the man in the right place at the right time (out of reach of the tidal wave but with a good *view?*), Ed sent an eyewitness report on the natural disaster in Connemara to the *Daily Mail*, and was in due course awarded a prize for Best New Journalist of the Year. His subsequent exposé of the 3 old biddies – 'GRAN THEFT' – also earned him great acclaim (at least among people who consider journalism something worth doing). Ed would never achieve equilibrium – but as journalists go, he was content.

His giant pumpkin had meanwhile floated bravely out to sea with the misidentified mango ('Dwarf Melon') speared on its stalk. Together, they spread their seeds across the globe.

'. . . Stolen items recovered after the ladies'
unfortunate demise included:

1,370 old-lady scarves
843 woolly jumpers, both old and new
799 dowdy blouses
678 dated skirts and dresses
619 unfashionable undies
445 galumphy shoes
421 pairs gaudy earrings (clip-on)
415 unbecoming hats
394 puffy coats and jackets
369 pairs support hose
332 imitation gold necklaces
236 pairs gardening gloves
167 bulging handbags
38 geraniums
25 umbrellas
20 handy pocket-sized plastic fold-up
see-through rain hats
18 hot-water bottles
10 wigs
8 fur coats
4 cassette tapes Irish accordion music
3 wheely baskets
1 fire extinguisher'

(Ed's article)

Eloïse's grandmother's tired old bones settled into a deep-sea cave, where what remained of her was nibbled by a dogfish. But a page of her poem on widowhood somehow survived and was later discovered floating off the coast of Newfoundland:

> *All of life a piecing-together*
> *Photofits of names, faces.*
> *A looking after, looking back.*
> *Bothered by insects and the*
> *Ill-fit of clothes.*
> *At times*
> *The urge to know*
> *Colours things.*
> *But it is as nothing to this*
> *Slow silent crawl.*
> *Poor further me etching this fate.*

THE END

'AND I ONLY AM ESCAPED ALONE TO TELL THEE.' Job

The drama's done. Why then here does any one step forth?
-- Because one did survive the wreck.

APPENDIX A

ANOTHER list of about 20,000 dormant prewar accounts is to be published by the Swiss Bankers' Association in October, continuing what one Swiss newspaper yesterday dubbed "an historic-striptease" to return the unclaimed assets of Holocaust victims.

The list of 1,872 non-Swiss names, published in *The Times* and other newspapers worldwide yesterday, as well as on the Internet, is the product of the banks' own search. A helpline set up to handle inquiries was besieged yesterday by Holocaust survivors and claimants.

Greville Janner, chairman of the Holocaust Educational Trust which pressed the banks to release details, said: "The telephone has not stopped ringing for a second . . . it will create an appalling workload for the banks."

APPENDIX B

As someday it may happen that a victim must be found,
I've got a little list, I've got a little list
Of society offenders who might well be underground
And who never would be missed, who never will be missed.
There's the pestilential nuisances who write for autographs,
All people who have flabby hands and irritating laughs,
All children who are up on dates and floor you with 'em flat,
All persons who in shaking hands shake hands with you like *that*,
And all third persons who on spoiling tête-à-têtes insist –
They'd none of them be missed, none of them be missed.

> He's got 'em on the list
> He's got 'em on the list
> And they'd none of them be missed,
> None of them be missed.

There's the banjo serenader and the others of his race
And the piano-organist, I've got *him* on the list,
And the people who eat peppermint and puff it in your face –
They never would be missed, they never would be missed.
And the idiot who praises with enthusiastic tone
All centuries but this and every country but his own,
And the lady from the provinces who dresses like a guy
And who doesn't think she dances but would rather like to try.

And that singular anomaly, the lady novelist –
I don't think she'd be missed, I'm sure she'd not be missed!

    He's got her on the list

    He's got her on the list

    And I don't think she'd be missed

    I'm sure she'd not be missed . . .

        (as sung by Ko-Ko, the Lord High Executioner,

           in *The Mikado* by Gilbert and Sullivan)

APPENDIX C

WORST DISASTERS IN THE BRITISH ISLES:

Disaster	Number killed	Date
Famine/Typhus (Ireland)	1,500,000–3,000,000	1846–51
Black Death	800,000	1347–50
Influenza	225,000	1918
Circular storm (Channel)	c. 8,000	1703
Smog (London)	3,500–4,000	1952
Flood (Severn Estuary)	c. 2,000	1606
Bombing (London)	1,436	1941
Single ship (*Royal George*)	c. 800	1782
Riot (anti-Catholic; London)	565 (min.)	1780
Mining (Wales)	439	1913
Terrorism (Lockerbie)	270	1988
Burst dam (Yorkshire)	250	1864
Railway collision	227	1915
Fire (London Bridge)	3,000	1212
Fire (single building; Exeter)	188	1887
Panic (Sunderland)	183	1883
Offshore oil platform (*Piper Alpha*)	167	1988
Landslide (Aberfan)	144	1966

Explosion (Notts.)	134	1918
Nuclear reactor (Windscale)	c. 100	1957
Submarine (Liverpool Bay)	99	1939
Tornado (Tay Bridge collapse)	75	1879
Helicopter (Shetland Isles)	45	1986
Road (coach crash, N.Yorks.)	33	1975
Lightning (annual total)	31	1914
Yacht racing (Fastnet)	19	1979
Avalanche (Lewes)	8	1836
Mountaineering (Cairn Gorm)	6	1971
Earthquake (London)	2	1580

REFERENCES

Quoted in the Text (with page numbers)

vii *Moby Dick*, Herman Melville (1851)

2 *Documents of the Holocaust*, ed. Yitzhak Arad, Yisrael Gutman and Abraham Margaliot (1981/1990)

3 *Night*, Elie Wiesel (1958)

7 *Ants Bees and Wasps*, Sir John Lubbock (1929)

18 *Life*, Count Lyof N. Tolstoy (trans. Isabel F. Hapgood, 1889)

19 *Bumblebees*, Oliver E. Prŷs-Jones and Sarah A. Corbet (1991)

20 *(Ditto)*

31 *Extinction*, Thomas Bernhard (trans. David McLintock, 1995)

35 *The Bee Craftsman*, H. J. Wadey (1943)

36 *Seashells*, S. Peter Dance (1989)

51 *Bumblebees (see above)*

52 *Ants Bees and Wasps (see above)*

55 *Don Giovanni*, Mozart/Lorenzo Da Ponte (trans. William Murray, 1961)

55 *Daily Telegraph*

59 *One, Two, Three with Ant and Bee*, Angela Banner (1958)

61 *Bumblebees (see above)*

62 *The Life of the Bee*, Maurice Maeterlinck (trans. Alfred Sutro, 1901)

64 *Guardian*

77 *The Easy Way to Tree Recognition*, John Kilbracken (1983)

77 *King Lear*, William Shakespeare (1605)

78 *The Easy Way to Tree Recognition (see above)*

79 *Moby Dick (see above)*

82 *The Holocaust* (from *The History of the Jews*), Paul Johnson (1996) (Penguin 60s edition)

83 *The Natural History of Selborne*, Gilbert White (1788/9)

87 *Moby Dick (see above)* – quoting from Darwin, *Voyage of a Naturalist*

91 'At Castle Boterel', Thomas Hardy (1913)

104 *The Natural History of Selborne (see above)*

106 *Bumblebees (see above)*

107 *Mushrooms*, Dr Mirko Svrček (1975)

113 *The Bee Craftsman (see above)*

114 *The Famine Decade*, ed. John Killen (1995)

115 *Stolen Continents: The Indian Story*, Ronald Wright (1992)

119 *The Famine Decade (see above)*

120 *Connemara,* Tim Robinson (1990)

121 *The Humble-bee*, F. W. L. Sladen (1912)

123 *The 'Mary Celeste' and Other Tales of the Sea*, J. G. Lockhart (1958)

127 *Moby Dick (see above)*

127 *Independent on Sunday* (series on learning to swim)

128 *The Famine Decade (see above)*

135 *A Sentimental Journey*, Laurence Sterne (1768)

137 *The Bee Craftsman (see above)*

138 (*Ditto*)

140 *The Natural History of Selborne (see above)*

141 'In the Seven Woods', W. B. Yeats (1902)

142 *Seven Woods Trail and the Family Trail*, Coole Park guidebook, by Tim O'Connell (1994)

143 'To be Carved on a Stone at Thoor Ballylee', W. B. Yeats (1921)

143 'Among School Children', W. B. Yeats (1928)

146   *Connemara (see above)*

148   *The Bee Craftsman (see above)*

150   *The Humble-bee (see above)*

153   *Ants Bees and Wasps (see above)*

154   *The Bee Craftsman (see above)*

156   *The New Guinness Book of World Records 1996*, ed. Peter Matthews (1996)

158   *The Natural History of Selborne (see above)*

158   *Name This Bird*, Eric Fitch Daglish (1934)

160   *(Ditto)*

169   *Seashells (see above)*

174   *The Hockey Handbook*, Lloyd Percival (1992)

177   *Casablanca*, dir. Michael Curtiz (1940)

180   *King Lear (see above)*

181   *Madeline*, Ludwig Bemelmans (1958)

185   *The Ocean Almanac*, Robert Hendrickson (1992) – account of a tsunami

186   *The Ocean Almanac (see above)*

189   *Connemara (see above)*

193   *Documents of the Holocaust (see above)*

198   *The Bee Craftsman (see above)*

202   *The Ocean Almanac (see above)*

208   *Moby Dick (see above)*

209   *The Times*

210   *The Mikado*, Gilbert and Sullivan

212   *The New Guinness Book of World Records 1996 (see above)*

Additional Sources (not directly quoted)

The Song of Hiawatha, Henry Wadsworth Longfellow (1855)

How to Grow Giant Vegetables, Colin Bowcock (1979)